Also by Ross Feld
ONLY SHORTER
YEARS OUT
PHILIP GUSTON
PLUM POEMS

A NOVEL BY

ROSS FELD

Shapes Mistaken

NORTH POINT PRESS 1989
San Francisco

Copyright © 1989 by Ross Feld
Printed in the United States of America

The author gratefully acknowledges
support from the National Endowment for
the Arts and the Ohio Arts Council during
the writing of this book.

LIBRARY OF CONGRESS
CATALOGING-IN-PUBLICATION DATA
Feld, Ross, 1947–
  Shapes mistaken: a novel / by Ross Feld.
  p.   cm.
  ISBN: 0-86547-367-6
  I. Title.
PS3556.E454S53   1989
813'.54—dc19   88-37465

*For Ellen, Aaron
and, in memory, P.G.*

Shapes Mistaken

APRIL

I

Before proceeding to Sid's affair, Shapes first drove across the river in weak afternoon light to the restaurant in the D-Lux Motel, where he planned to stuff himself on lion's head and that way be sure to get at least one decent meal for the day. He'd phoned ahead from the store so the Hings would be ready: Aahs of welcome, a little bit of talk about the premature heat, then Henry Hing sweeping an arm through the room, offering any deep-backed seat in the house. Followed by ice water, hot tea, and ultimately Frankie—chef and eldest son—marching out with the burly meatballs, his mother shyly hanging back behind.

But this was the absolutely worst moment, the one they all could have done without, failing restaurants being stressful places. The anxious-to-please looks, the too-hearty praise. (Sidney, his one and only time, hadn't handled it well: "Like they were next going to serve up their virgin daughter! Good *night*.") Thankfully Poppa Henry was always there to re-take the reins, to pat his only customer's back with a small-boned practiced hand and see that the rest of the family went gliding back to the kitchen . . . leaving Shapes, a chopstick in each fist, to break open the tennis-ball-sized things and go at it.

Which was now how it was exactly: Shapes arrived, conversed, was seated (a table in the middle of the empty room, his back to the large window) and served, and ultimately ate, spooning an eye of reddish broth onto the glossy rice in the porcelain bowl with the tail-biting dragons in chase on the side, nesting a meatball-chunk atop that—much too much food for only one person, but did he care? If he avoided arriving around lunch or dinner and stuck like now to the late afternoons, the privacy turned him into a pasha. Naturally he worried for the Hings, inept businessmen like himself, and felt he should be doing more recommending of the D-Lux. But not quite yet—as he slipped off his shoes under the table and a shoulder-heating angle of sunlight poured into the room.

In his defense, there was the one lunch here with Sid Telscher and also once a dinner with Elise, the last time she was up to visit from Florida, her comprehensive ass just about fitting into one of the lyre-shaped chairs. Shapes that evening did the complete ordering: no consultation and no moderation, the more food, the less talk. Usually Elise felt the need to account for every minute of her every distant day—but look! here were the cold noodles! and in they'd have to dig: Jack Sprat and wife, Elise's tiny dancing wet black eyes, that still lovely smile (drooping once, as the Hings kept bringing, but only momentarily, a shame able to be eaten through). As kids, when she was as narrow as Shapes was still, in places like Fort Lee and Hackensack after seeing the Dorseys or Stan Kenton (her musical taste, not his) at one or another of the trying-too-hard Jersey theaters, back then they used to feed in roadhouses together on half raw steaks, seated biceps to biceps in leather half-moon booths the color of artery blood—sawing away, two knives at a single slab, "No, silly, look what . . . , don't!" as she'd reach over, pull the fork away from Shapes's lips and force his wrist back to the table, then delicately edge away the char.

No Jack Sprat, he loved the taste of fat, though for Elise's sake he made it seem that he didn't trim his meat out of simple inattention; it served her needs to think of him as in a general fog. Once at a buffet supper he contentedly ate a double portion of shrimp and clam gumbo, ignoring a grittiness to the broth—as the hostess responded to compliments on the food with a frazzled sigh of triumph: amazed, she said, it had all come off. She had run out of tomatoes; Herb forgot to pick up the wine; and while she cooked, a glass hurricane lamp that sat on top of one of the cabinets had fallen onto the stove and shattered—some mess! Elise had them out of there as soon as politely possible; parked outside the first all-night store they found—in the north Bronx—she forced slice after slice of Wonder Bread on him, nibbling at some herself though she'd eaten only salad, smiling at his comments about a grislier death from constipation as IRT trains like rehearsing thunder made brief stops at the elevated station overhead.

Shapes looked at his watch, which plainly urged, Eat faster! Because today's lion's head wasn't the best ever, and because one or another smooth Hing face intermittently appeared behind the glass inserts of the quilted kitchen doors, he didn't mind speeding it up. (The faster he chewed and swallowed, though, the louder the sound in his ears—a long grating rustle that eventually dwindled.)

Yet better to be watched than to have to do the watching, to have to sit facing the window and observe exactly what a motel entailed. Through the glass one afternoon he'd seen the private carter's truck roll up and Poppa Henry and the driver engaging in discussion, a disagreement apparently. Soon Henry was trotting across the parking lot into one of the nearby rooms, its door already wide open. He reappeared pulling a discolored mattress by its side handles. Giving the truck's klaxon one terrible bop, the driver stepped from the cab and shook his head no. Henry stopped, walked around the mattress, a hand on its edge to find a more manageable purchase, and again began dragging it toward the truck.

By then Mrs. Hing was involved—cutting across the parking lot, gesticulating violently. Shapes had never seen an Oriental woman so exposed in rage, but here was the old lady grabbing hold of the other corner of the mattress and tugging it with all her strength back *toward* the room. While husband and wife contested and the mattress's big dumb rectangularity bowed and buckled like a drunken horse, the dumpster driver took a few dainty steps back toward the truck as if knowing Shapes was his audience, swung up into the cab, and drove off.

Just today, too, driving in, Shapes had noticed a Tasteebread van parked in front of one of the rooms—like a modern twist on the salacious old milkman jokes. And months ago, leaving the restaurant, hadn't he for a moment been positive he was encountering his son-in-law arriving here? a persimmon Toyota about as disgraceful as the one the kids drove? the man behind the wheel wearing the same green or loden Irish tweed hat Bennett kept on his head well into spring? Shapes in his Volvo had stopped to clear his grumbling ears—a finger's worth of suction—before getting on the road. The Toyota, about to turn into the D-Lux, at the last second seemed to change its mind and went on past. All Shapes could make of the other person in the car was a descending shoulder ducking from sight.

Not Bennett, he rapidly realized—too tall, too erect a frame. Yet at the sight of the catastrophic orange car, the Irish hat, the ducking shoulder—and feeling himself borne up by a powerful, confusing surge—Shapes's hand had risen in an excited wave. An *encouraging* wave, he had to admit; his chest had tingled like a drumhead. Even now, staring at one of the miniature orange trees and the gold

Chinese characters on the sheath wrapped around the roots, he could guiltily taste the amount of *welcome* in that wave.

And though obviously it was "better" that it hadn't been Bennett, that Bennett was so lawful domestically, something in Shapes still wouldn't have minded *fearing* his only son-in-law a little bit. Fathers should be slightly cowed by these usurpers, threatened by their recklessness, the way they forged new laws through fracture and reattachment. With Bennett it never got off on that foot. Shapes and Elise were probably too grateful for the boy. Amy had seemed destined (especially in Elise's eyes; not a good relationship there) to be a spinster. Average-nice looks, but the problem was her "selfishness." Her "procrastinations." Her "sarcastic attitude to everything." No wonder she beat back boys in droves. Except for this one skinny kid—who flew against the wind to love her and pressed her to marry a year after college and bred children out of her. And then in essence collapsed around himself, all initiative gone.

Now, though, that Bennett worked at the store, he did seem slightly more lively, which was good. Sarcastic all the time (Amy's influence) and watchful of—and not very friendly to—Iris (which had its advantages: it kept down Iris's occasional filchings—stamps, stationery, pens, small merchandise), but at least more or less out of his bog. Until just recently he'd served as the paid director of a county arts consortium, dependent on grants the government no longer was granting and whose one independent moneymaker—a string quartet in residence at Vassar—had just this winter had its cellist killed in an auto crash and was in the process of disbanding.

So if it only *had* been Bennett in that car, turning into the D-Lux. To see some life, to see the poor kid begin to feel it all out before he woke up too late and found that he must compress. (Look at Sidney: politics now that he was nearing sixty—though really wanting to see order *mocked*, made trivial and cynical and open to manipulation, seeking some late intricacy truly intricate enough to keep him webbed-up and hidden from death.) But it hadn't been Bennett: too tall behind the wheel, and someone even slenderer. All these matchbox-toy Japanese cars resembled one another anyway.

Done with his meal, Shapes got to his feet quickly, crushing his napkin; occasionally the Hings would have a surprise for him—a special noodle dish, a sweet—but today he simply didn't have time. Out on cue swung Mrs. Hing, chin ahead of herself, a Wheatena-colored cardigan draped over her turquoise tunic-suit (the room had been absurdly cold ever since his arrival). Inspecting the serving bowl and his plate: "Eat so quick?"

"Very scrumptious. Tell Frankie for me."

"Tea? No more tea?"

Shapes was opening the pouch of his wallet. Lion's head didn't appear on the menu and was made specially for him only because he'd once been curious. The price therefore was something he himself had been obliged to set and could now not alter. He plucked out a ten, a five, and normally would have fooled with the money a little—rolling the bills into a tube or stashing them somewhere odd on the table, anything to tone down the ceremoniousness. But today he let it go. Showing up at the dinner any later than the fruit cup or soup would upset Sidney. The old lady however was already crying out a summons in Chinese.

Shapes tried to head Frankie off. "Unless that look in your eyes means you're finally going to give me the recipe, I don't want you." The boy grinned but didn't stop, and eyeing Shapes's tux, said: "Look at *you*, man."

"A function I have to go to. What?"

Frankie was holding out a wiggling open palm: "Car keys, lemme'. Start your car, get the air-conditioning cold. Come *on*!"

"What come on? Come on yourself!" Shapes moved rapidly around Frankie with a wriggling goodbye wave, thrust toward the ceiling's brown stipple of asbestos. Something discomforting here each and every time, a price for the pleasure. "Start your car . . ."!

Abjection was snot. They could feed and fawn over him all they liked within the restaurant, their proper zone. But that was all; niceness wasn't goodness, and every thoughtless, casual substitution of the two cost a person dearly. For years Shapes had been a salesman, had sold pianos for Sidney Telscher; now with his own business—not pianos: audio—he was still in retail, he was still serving the public. In other words, a lifetime spent being nice—and never in the process having to be good. Oh, Shapes knew a thing or two about this terrible abjection snare. At least poor Poppa Henry wasn't in the lobby holding the door.

Shapes marched to his Volvo in flat, threadbare light. He craved depth the way Elise craved chocolate, yet the dusk was stingy: a shiny sky, smoother perhaps, but as close; and it was only when he arrived on the other side of the river, at the banquet restaurant's parking lot, sitting in the car and looking for a moment through the windshield, that he saw some faint stars starting to struggle out. Some hint of space.

The Telschers' Mercedes was already parked, alone of its breed that Shapes saw. Enduring ghetto instincts suggested to Shapes that they should have driven the Olds instead. Of course Sid never would have done so. Shapes, driving by Sid's carport just this morning, found him with a squeeze bottle of Blue Poly, a sponge, a bucket, and what looked like two new chammies, all ready to go at the Mercedes. As soon as Shapes stopped, Telscher took an immediate interest in a suds runnel.

Usually the kidding would be over how Sid dared wash a car this lush himself. But the fresher opportunity was irresistible today. Shapes had rolled down the window and leaned forward against the Volvo's steering wheel, peering through the windshield, appealing to the skies:

"Morty, oh, Morty. *Kik arop fun dem himl!*"

Sidney squeegeed with an edge of the brick-like sponge. "You promised—no giving me a hard time." Morton had been the eldest, most impressive of the three Telscher boys: a volunteer in Spain with the Lincoln Brigade, wounded at Belchite, later a dry cleaner, staunch and Stalinist, dead now a few years.

Again Shapes had leaned across the wheel: "Re*pub*licans!—and not like *you* knew from, either!"

Sidney worked daintily around the hood emblem. "The world, my friend, changes."

"I feel for it, believe me. Everyone blames the poor world."

"But you're still coming."

"Would I miss it?" Shapes had patted his breast pocket where the ticket, fifty dollars a plate, stood. "I'm picking the suit up at noon."

How was it that all these "function" restaurants had identical configurations, cramped at the mouth and at the neck—one person designed them all? Hunky wooden doors with handles like scepters opened with alarming ease on a dark small foyer, a gloomy reservations desk. (The thin middle-aged woman who took Shapes's ticket there indicated the coatroom. When he said, "In this weather?" she answered seriously: "The ladies have furs, sir." Unhappily he was beginning to forget.) Narrow wainscotted passages. Men's and ladies' rooms. An office marked Private—and Shapes all the while making flattened way for leavers (God forbid there was a fire), finally arriving at a wider area of brighter lights, fake flowers, an easel supporting a corrugated signboard.

Once his ears had adjusted to the thud of the band on the other side of the white doors, it felt good to be somewhere other than those pinched hallways. Shapes found his placecard, Table Two, which when he located it was half empty: no Sid, no Doris. The two middle-aged couples who did sit there reassured him though that, yes, this was the Telschers' table. They were off somewhere, circulating. Shapes dropped his camera bag on one of the empty chairs.

The soup bowl at his setting was cool to the touch. Nor were Sid's and Dorie's giving off steam. They could be gone a long time yet.

One of the women at the table, a small plump blonde wearing eyeglasses with designer initials etched in at the corner of one lens, asked him, "Is Mrs. Shapes with you?" As he answered "Unfortunately, no, she isn't," he registered the woman's husband settling significantly against her upper arm.

In the uncomfortable silence following, Shapes tasted the soup. (Looking at it more carefully, he saw it was vichyssoise.) How many times, back in his piano-selling days—at receptions, at concerts, at the sales dinners the manufacturers used to throw at the swankiest spots—had he been taken for a widower? For he'd always show up alone. Preceded by days of unseen drama. A social occasion would loom and activate all the stages. First Elise would declare: Definitely not going. Then maybe. Then no again: nothing to wear. Then a minimum two-day depression, a spill of loathing, hatred of herself but more of him, for having put her through this, for his slobby sociability that got them invited in the first place. At that point a new dress box might appear, leaning up against one side of her closet—but this a false sign, a premature bud, because the box would be returned the next day and they'd be back to square one.

Now and then they'd actually get as far as the car before Elise balked. Never with tears or bewailings but with a dignified put-outness instead, the car rising dolefully on its springs as she left it, clippering back into the house in her dressy high-heeled suede sandals. Once or twice Shapes had been able to bring her as far as the parking lot—followed by looks of befuddlement behind other windshields as the Shapeses were seen leaving before anything was under way. He used to imagine the conversations in those cars. The man: "It's sad." The woman: "The poor thing." He: "To make it worse, she's basically good-looking. Beautiful face." She: "Pleasant, I'd say pleasant." "That's got to be something hormonal, doesn't it?" "Who I feel sorry for really is *him*—he's the one with the hands full." "Does he, ooh!" "That isn't nice—what would you do if *I* looked that way?" Yet it taught Shapes a lesson about shame—

something he had a tendency to overvalue. Shame, it turned out, wasn't very choosy, or even all that strickenly individual. Instead it was a group activity, with group dilutions: after you securely got other people to think how awful you must feel, you didn't actually have to—or at least not quite so much.

Someone over his shoulder was kissing his cheek.

"We saw you come in but were being introduced and couldn't get away." Doris took the seat beside him. "It's about time you're here." Wiping lipstick off him with her thumb, she looked flushed, but at the same time underused, like the groom's mother at a wedding. "We need you. Or at least I do."

Shapes pulled his camera from the bag on the other seat. "And where's His Nibs?"

"Rightcheer—if you mean me."

Shapes, swiveling adroitly, was able to catch Telscher fat with the flash, dazzling him into raising crossed hands to hide his face. One of the other men at the table called out "Good shot!" and Shapes noted, "Like your average Just-Indicted pose," as blinking Sidney ("Very nice, very nice—now I'm blind") took his seat.

After selling his piano business in Manhattan and moving from Midwood in Brooklyn to the condo in Goshen; after a year and a half of meticulous newspaper reading, of joining a synagogue and becoming active in the Men's Club and of volunteering to organize publicity for the local Philharmonia and of dropping into Shapes's store mum as a Trappist (the silent partner thing pushed a bit far)— after all this grueling leisure, Telscher not surprisingly started to unravel. Dorie had another story for Shapes each time she saw him. Living right there himself, the eternal neighbor, he'd seen much of it himself: flagrantly unnecessary appointments with medical specialists, impossible morning ill humors, fifteen pairs of shoes in two months, none of them fitting "just right," so none ever worn twice.

Finally, at his eldest son's urging, Sid had taken a look at local politics. The problem was that a Democrat hadn't won a local position in seventeen years. Yet, screwing up his courage, Sid made a call to a selectman he knew from the Philharmonia board and lived to tell the tale. *These* Republicans, he told anyone who'd listen (and said to Shapes over and over), were a good group: congenial, less crusty than expected, no overt Birchers, even a few Jews seeded into the ranks. Golf had been played with the county chairman twice already, and both times Sidney wasn't allowed so much as to tip the shoeshine boy in the clubhouse. It happened that, after fourteen years at it, the woman who currently was town auditor planned to retire with her husband to California. Since in the township nomination equaled election, soon after choosing its slate the party threw itself a dinner dance, exulting in the neatness of it all. For weeks now Sidney had worn the startled look of someone kissed unexpectedly on the lips.

Shapes's flash unit signaled re-readiness, winking its small red eye. He snapped everyone at the table and was snapped in return—sitting beside the Telschers—by the woman wearing the initialed glasses. The camera, these lenses, this flash and musette bag—Elise had presented it all to him as a gift-package for his birthday, handed over almost six months to the day before announcing that she was going to live in Florida to see if a last little bit of money couldn't be squeezed out of the eastern coast for S & S Properties and Management, the firm in which she'd risen from bookkeeper to office manager to partner after old man Showalter's death. Nor, she said, did she think it was reasonable to expect Shapes to drop his life and job and friends and concerts to exile himself down there with her.

By then she'd been closing in on two hundred pounds; at certain places on her scalp the hair thinned perilously. The queen-sized bed in the bedroom was hers alone, insomniac nights spent with a window open no matter the weather and Barry Gray, Long John Knebel, or any all-night talk show oozing companionably from the radio. Shapes had relocated to his daughter's empty room upstairs—a garret, the ceiling of which Amy had papered-over with pictures scissored from *Life* and fixed with clear varnish in the seventh grade. In the mornings Shapes lay studying the yellowed montage, mostly of animals and flower fields, mountains at sunset, very few people (unless with a distorted or funny expression), cherishing this ceiling, the blotter for most of Amy's life's-portion of creative ambition. He occupied the room beneath it respectfully, monkishly, feeling capable of floating up within it; few nightmares and fewer dirty dreams in that bed, and at dawn he scrupulously whisked off anything the frilly night table held: his glasses, a book, a tumbler of water.

He had turned an agreeably purified fifty-three up there in the picture-filled room, and had come downstairs to find Elise dressed, ready to go to work (she took an earlier train) but awaiting his appearance. Wrapped cartons were on the kitchen table.

"I thought with this, not like the Instamatic, you could really have a wonderful hobby."

The camera: a box through which to view the world. A squint machine. The gift of someone accustomed to squeezing into things—but horrendously inappropriate for someone like Shapes, a present contrary in every way to what he felt was the direction of his soul. Although, of course, he thanked her, he'd felt like crying.

A steady stream of people arrived at Table Two, brought by the county chairman for the Telschers to meet. Shapes obligingly slid his chair ever leftward to make room, and in the midst of one particularly bad clog rose minus his camera. He caught Doris's eye. "The little boy's room," he mouthed to her and with a bent arm and knee prowed a smiling path out of the crowd.

As he was skirting the dance floor's edge without a destination, someone he didn't know—a woman—grabbed at his hand. A moment later he was in the middle of the floor, dancing, her hair pressed against his temple. Someone roughly his age was his impression (this without a good frontal look at her). Graceful, lessons probably, maybe a widow who semi-brazenly came to these things (just grabbing out like that!) for the opportunity to dance. Words soaked in the sweetwood smell of liquor were blowing past Shapes's ear:

"Heard that Joe-Bo was picked up last night again? The same old thing."

Dispensed by the unlikeliness of his being here at all, Shapes thought why not? "DWI?"

"*Blind*. Though no one's supposed to know yet—or ever. Van Vlack will *have* to do something now, something disciplinary. Knowing him though, he'll put it off as long as possible."

"We're not going to hold our breaths," Shapes agreed.

"Even a little decisiveness would be good for him."

"For Joe-Bo," said Shapes.

"For Van Vlack."

"Also I'm sure for Joe-Bo."

"All these years of Mary trying to keep it quiet. Some of us who know her well and are close, we always *knew* that it wasn't anything he had under control . . ." The music had stopped ("Three Coins in the Fountain"—but only when it was done did Shapes really hear it) and the band then was slow to resume. Maybe if he didn't step back she'd dance again. But no, she was pushing away with a farewell hand-squeeze. "See you!"

Frosted blond-gray hair, reddish face, long neck, stub at the hip.

Shapes gallantly bowed.

Telscher was gone when Shapes got back to the table and no one at all was talking to Dorie, who fiddled with her salad. She was easily enough lifted to her feet. Out on the floor Shapes tried fitting his feet to the notes of a sluggard "Sentimental Journey," but Doris stopped him with a palm's worth of pressure, locking them both into the rhythm before relinquishing the lead.

"Doing okay?" Shapes asked her. "Holding up? Seems to be a friendly function."

Doris brushed vervelessly at his lapel. "This is handsome. Have I seen it before?"

"Do I own a tux? It's a rental."

"*Really* want to know how I'm doing? *Terrible*, that's how."

"The meeting new people? You'll pick it up. It's only difficult at first, and then you'll find the depth." Shapes couldn't resist. Twenty-five years ago, on the beach at Riis Park after going to get Melorols for the kids, Telscher—out of the blue and in a chafed mumble—had confided to Shapes as they walked back to the blankets with the ice creams: "You maybe find this with Elise, I don't know . . . Dorie is very—*particular* . . . I'm not allowed to go too deep—she says it hurts her . . ." Slowed by the sand, with fully occupied hands, Shapes never had experienced such a sense of sapping disadvantage. Sidney went on: "I thought she'd adapt, especially after having the babies. But 'deep' to her gets shallower and shallower to me. One day she's not going to want me even to—I'm not, you know, *complaining* . . ."

Nor was it the last thing of that kind Shapes would be let in on. One slow afternoon in the piano store, Sid was on the verge of sharing the devotional words he and Doris kissed goodnight to in bed. For what if he died—or Doris did—before they woke in the morning? They'd never see each other again!—and Sid was about to relate the dizzyingly private words when Shapes barked *Please!* and hurried away. He'd felt ever since then that friends should only be painted pictures of paradise. They could easily guess all the rest, the common run of tears and shit, but who said the sinking choose to embrace?

"You're capable," Shapes encouraged Dorie. "You can do it."

"Well so says you, and thank you, but I know I'm not. This is a real problem, Charlie—it's going to get me *and* Sidney in trouble, *tonight*." Doom lowered her voice. "The chairman's wife—Van Vlack's wife—I don't remember her name. I *can't* remember it. When I first met her, and two other times when Van Vlack introduced her to someone else—three separate times tonight it's gone in and then right out of my head."

"Wouldn't 'Mrs. Van Vlack' suffice?"

"No, she's that seriously informal type. Is it Fuzzy? *Fritzy?* Something F. Watch," Doris lamented, "it's probably something like

Jean. What do I do if I have to introduce her?" Then she admitted to telling a few other people from Crescent Hill about tonight: "Not that I expect them to come, but they were nice enough to buy tickets"—Shapes knowing it pained both Dorie and Sidney to think he might ever suspect they had other friends as well, that they'd thereby be judged unreliables, not the secured fortress whose doors swung open only for him. "I'd normally go ask Sid—but here and now? I don't want him worrying, of all times, about my incompetence."

"I could ask him."

"He'd know something was up. He's the opposite of me: when he gets agitated, he thinks sharper. And it isn't like there's exactly a way to avoid her—she's everywhere; these things are *work* for the wives. Nice predicament, huh? Doris Telscher, Screwing Up Again."

Shapes told her she was worrying needlessly, she'd have to introduce nobody: "There's a general assumption of belonging."

Doris was unconvinced. "You're such a good dancer. You always were."

Shapes had an idea.

"I'll prove it to you. These people are strangers to me, yes? We're just going to dance, not say one word—but now *everyone* is going to say hello to me. All these strangers who've never seen me before. Ready? Starting . . . right . . . *now!*"

"Charlie—"

Shapes smiled *seriously*—the gunned engine of his Volvo serving as a mental model, or the commercial he'd passed this morning while walking down the TV aisle in the store: sixteen Krazy-Glued plates holding sixteen horses up off the ground—a width, a gleam put into it; a smile thrown past Dorie's head like a newly forged rivet.

The first "Hey, how's the boy?"—from a bullet-headed man dancing with a woman in a lemon dress immediately to their left, *someone Shapes had never seen before*—Doris unfortunately missed. But not the next one: "Good to see ya." She gasped and giggles came up out of her like bubbles escaping a dunked tire.

"See?" Shapes whispered.

Another dancing couple accidentally collided with them. The man, after a smiled apology to Shapes's turned head, added, "Fun tonight, isn't it? Better than the last few," before moving off. Shapes looked down proudly at Doris—who in turn, with excited little slaps, began batting at his shoulders:

"I've *got* it! *Anne-Grace!*"

He prolonged the stunt a little longer, for his own amusement, broadcasting smiles, receiving chin-shakes or hellos in return—but only when the music stopped did Doris have anything to say about it directly. "How did you do that? How'd you know?"

"You gauge the crowd, whether they're amenable. A *fillin'*, like Sid's father used to say."

Doris wouldn't have it. "It's *you*. It's how you"—but here the band broke in, starting up again. "Marie (My Heart Is Breaking)." Doris's face dropped once more:

"Not Anne-*Grace*—I'm so hopeless! Anne-*Marie!*" Relaxed, she took on a goony expression. "Of all of us from the old gang, Charlie, you were the only one who ever really knew what to *do*. I felt this always."

Shapes frowned, moving her into step. "No one knows what to do ever."

"Even as a kid you weren't afraid to *take* what you knew you needed. You have natural *timing*."

Embarrassed, Shapes hummed the melody aggressively, bobbing his chin at the downbeats: "Ma-*rie* . . . dah dah dah-*da*-dah—all you have to do is not forget this song."

She looked around. "Where's Sidney? He has to hear what happened."

Taking? Timing?

They found Sid standing behind his chair, in the midst of more introductions. (The party chairman, next to him, reserved a moment to nod to the band for his wife's name-song—smiling but over a subface of *not now*.) Sidney drew Doris close—"Here she is!"—addressing a couple: a man with a Lincoln beard—no moustache—who was bent nearly double upon a pair of aluminum half-crutches; and his dark-haired woman companion (though Shapes didn't get a good look at her until a waiter setting down an entrée forced her to make way). "Dorie, this is Justice Mackey, Mister Mackey."

Flustered by the posture, the canes, Doris bent low to shake the man's hand. "Pleased to meet you, Judge."

Sid and the chairman exchanged glances, and the chairman said gently to Doris, "*Mrs.* Mackey is our magistrate. Roueysdale. Get caught speeding down their Main Street one afternoon and you'll meet her again one night the same week. No backlogs on *her* calendar! And bring your checkbook."

Doris went a brackish color. A better, more selfless friend would have created a diversion, stepping up to introduce himself, but Shapes stayed as he was. He knew this woman. From the store. But so far the judge/wife hadn't recognized him. Then, looking his way—after a moment to place the face—she did and smiled, surprised. A quip from Sid in the meantime had loosened the knot and let everyone disperse in relief.

A judge! Despite his meal at the D-Lux, Shapes found himself midway into the prime rib and cheerfully shaking plenty of salt over the cheesed potato and butter-sauced zucchini. A judge!

The first time she was in, he'd been by himself in the store (one of Bennett's days off and Iris out on one of her mysterious personal errands). What she believed she needed, she said—consulting a slip of paper—was a new . . . *cartridge?* For a *tone arm?* Shapes asked what kind of cartridge. She wasn't sure. "*Shure*, does it say there?" Together they looked at the paper. *Phono cartridge*—simply that. She owned an offset-and-copy shop in Kingston and explained that her "boys and girls" were fussy about their music, the radio not good enough for them. But unfortunately this was all the information they'd given her to go on.

She came around the counter when Shapes suggested she call. No rings on long fingers; a large nose, heavily tipped. An ink-blue suit, a white ruffled blouse, a red bow tie. Whitish stockings, pumps black as her hair. (As for underwear, his guess was: dramatic.) Unable to get through on the phone, she looked at her watch. She was running late; she'd have to come back. (A naughty corset even—a merrywidow?)

Then—only yesterday, expressly asking Iris for Shapes—she was back. This time in summer white, more simply dressed. Now she had the complete information—the brand of changer, what size cartridge it took. While he wrote up the sale, Shapes explained to her the store's optional wrinkle, the rent-to-own concept—and wondered aloud whether, in a place with the sort of floor vibrations a printing shop was subject to, a tapedeck might not be something she'd like to try instead. "Have two minutes?"

In the sound room he slipped in Iris's revolting Clapton (for the kids) and after a very little of that, his own Pollini Chopin. She listened, pearly nail polish on the hand resting atop one of the floor speakers, but had nothing to say during or after the music. Shapes rushed in heartily—"No problem! It's all right not to be sure"—and she ended up taking only the cartridge, as planned.

All right not to be sure. To a judge! Had she smiled to herself when he said that? He had no recollection. A soft belch lifted out of him, too much food, the lion's head and now the beef. Telscher, he noticed, was gone from the table again. "Let me see," Shapes said, rising, "if I can't also manage to sneak a few nice candids of our auditor-to-be." Doris broke off her conversation with one of the women at the table, sending him on his way with a smiling nod.

Shapes's camera and flash unit banged against his tie. Seeing this, most of those seated at the merrywidow's table on the other side of the room either hurried to swallow or put down their forks altogether. He fanned the air—"Please don't let your food get cold. I'll catch everyone later"—before squatting down to the side of the judge and inquiring how the cartridge had worked.

"Doll, this is Mr. Shapes." Even the correct pronunciation. "The man who sold me the needle for the record player." Twisting his twistedness without ceasing to eat—his right shoulder so low (chin and table only inches apart) that all he had to do was push food across the rim of the plate and to his lips—the spavined husband raised two fingers of greeting. "Well, our kids have stopped complaining, so the needle must be working. I'm sorry: the *cartridge*."

Above the returning band, loudness heaved like paint, Shapes said, "Any problems with installation?"

"I didn't fool with it. One of the boys put it on."

He aimed his chin at her untouched plate: "Vegetarian?"

Two of her fingers dropped gently to the man's bony wrist when the husband frumphed sourly at this. In the moue-ing way you'd speak to a poodle, she said, "Come on now—it's not stopping *you* any. You still get your three squares. You're not the dieting one, the one who's deprived—now are you? Noo you're not."

Shapes smiled. "Would you be strong enough for a short dance? Can I steal your wife away for five minutes tops, Mister Mackey?"

The husband patted the cushion of the chair his wife already was leaving: "Put all that stuff right here, on hers." Shapes did—letting the equipment down into the warm indentation. Immediately and blindly the husband covered it all with a proprietory hand.

"You see the same faces, year after year," said the judge/merrywidow to Shapes once they were on the dance floor. "That goes for the photographers too. I'm happy to see new blood. Are you—what's that called—freelance? As well as running your store?"

"My friends are the Telschers over at Table Two, the one you met who's running for—"

"Sidney? Of course—I think I vaguely knew he was in the electronics business. Maybe Monte Vee mentioned it to me. But I never put the two together."

(Did he feel a faint *cinch* at her waist? Was that at all possible?) "I'm just the amateur recording angel tonight, an old friend snapping away for the scrapbook."

"You *look* professional."

"Thank you. I tend to for some reason, I don't know why. Before the Sound Barn, Sid and I were in the piano business—"

"Here in the area?"

"This already was years ago. No, Manhattan. He was the boss, I was the employee, and even though in the beginning I had next to no sales—"

She interrupted again, sympathizing: "Everyone starts slowly."

"—Sid kept me on. Actually he had no choice. I'm his oldest friend. Another reason—he'd deny it, but it's the truth—is that—I don't know why—I *looked* so good on the bench demonstrating his instruments."

"All these talents. Take pictures. Play the piano."

"I *provoke* a piano: sounds come out, groans, begging me to stop. And look who's surprised at what someone else does. Is. You—a *judge*."

"The way you're a photographer. Part-time."

"I hate to think that I might have offered to send you an empty box or pre-date the warranty."

"Would you have done that?"

"I'm strictly a law-abider."

"Of course you are, you're a Republican."

"An independent," slightly tightening his grip on her. Something bony—not intrinsically her? A stay? Corset or not, how sincerely good she felt under hand. The moving heft of a largish female on a dance floor wasn't something foreign to Shapes. Still it was remarkable: the put-togetherness of a grown-up, dressed-up woman—yet here she was sliding into the channel of his decision (we go here, now we go there), allowing it not only for one or two ritual steps but for a hundred; going and swaying, blowing her scent around the floor. "Can I ask you, Judge Mackey, what your out-of-court name is—your first name—if that's all right? On the sales receipt you used your business's."

Soberly—nearly with ceremony—she told him it was Leona.

"I think there's, isn't there? a kind of German sausage . . ." (*What was he saying?*) "I'm Charles."

"And Mrs. Shapes—is she here tonight? I'd like to be introduced."

"I'm afraid she isn't."

Leona at that point shut her eyes. And continued to dance that way—boldly, considering that those on the dance floor or watching her from the tables were people who knew her, knew the state of her husband. Closed eyes. It had the effect of making Shapes feel even headier than during his stunt for Doris. "But when I *am* being a photographer"—causing her to open her eyes and look at him—"I do mostly nature studies. Indoor still lifes." A pause. "Figure studies."

Her back straightened. "You do these where?"

"In studio space in back of the store. Nothing fancy." (Nor, he guessed, difficult to set up quickly.)

"At night?"

"For the figure studies, yes"—and hearing himself next say "Would you be interested?" he felt as though he was landing from a height onto one foot. "I pay a fee to the models. The enormous windfall of twenty-five dollars per session."

No reaction from her. (*Shoot* instead of *session* would have sounded more professional.) Then she said: "On Tuesdays I have court and on Thursdays I do records. No, I probably couldn't do it."

Experiencing the sweet exhausted relief of a person snatched from his own stupidity, Shapes wore a carefully unaffiliated smile while walking her back to her table. But then Leona was saying: "If I *could*,

I'd call first. Would the day before be enough time? And anything special you'd want me to bring along? My makeup kit for instance?"

"Dandy."

"You'd remind me on the phone to bring that? If I could do it?"

The husband, slumped chin to chest and removed from the coffee-and-dessert chatter drifting across the table, looked dead in his chair. Leona leaned to stroke the short white curls at the bottom of his neck: "I'm back and I had a very nice dance. We're going to go soon, Doll. A nice snooze?"—as in the meantime Shapes lifted his camera and flash off the seat of her chair.

On Shapes's return, Doris gave a tetchy jump when he tapped at her shoulder. "Oh, good, you."

Shapes sat down. "You read all the magazines—you know about the lonely hours of the political wife."

"No, this time he was called to the phone. And you know that isn't it at all."

"Don't tell me. It's *not* Marie?"

With a foul look Doris reported that a few minutes ago someone she didn't know from a hole in the wall came over to compliment them—*she and Sidney*—on what good dancers they were. She stared meaningfully, angrily, at Shapes. Telscher never danced, he didn't know how; seeing Doris on the dance floor, this person obviously had mistaken Shapes for Telscher—and *that*, Doris bleakly summarized, was why everyone had said hello to him before. "It was *me* they were recognizing, the wife of the candidate. Most of them just met Sid tonight and probably forgot a minute later what his face looks like. They thought you were him. They were just extending a *courtesy*, saying hello."

Shapes stroked the back of her neck. "Politeness *depresses* you? I'd say make like a robber, scoop all of it you can."

Doris shook her head, unassuaged. "Not my point." She prodded an untouched petit four. "Anyone can be friendly. It's cheap. At something like tonight, they *have* to be."

Shapes made a pigeony sound of disapproval—his experience having been that nothing whatsoever was cheap. What had just happened with the judge (whatever that was) suggested that even cheap was expensive. But Dorie peevishly lifted his hand away from her shoulder.

"I'm glad that's what you think the point I'm making is. I don't like you when you decide to be dense, when you're stubborn and won't acknowledge what I'm trying to bring out. I know that God forbid you should ever believe in yourself—but can't I at least? I thought they were responding to what you . . . to your . . . *something*. Not *who* you are. But an openness, a *magic* they could feel."

"You're looking for problems," Shapes sighed. "People aren't already too magical to themselves? It's what causes half the heartache."

Dorie's attention however had caught on something else—on one of the men seated across the table, who was directing her by sign to turn around. Shapes turned too.

Just inside the doors of the banquet room Telscher stood waving. Both Shapes and Doris pointed at themselves, but Sid jabbed definitively at Shapes only.

In the vestibule, away from people, Sidney's words fell out in tight, soaked batches.

"Bennett. A call from Lauderdale."

Shapes didn't understand. "Bennett's in Florida? Oh, don't tell me he left Amy. Is it Amy? She all right? The girls?"

"A call *to* him—*from* Lauderdale."

"What?"

Now with frank weeping: "Elise—a heart attack, Charlie. She's gone."

JUNE

2

Bennett tried keeping away from the front windows, afraid that he'd watch like a dog who jumps on the couch and mournfully noses apart the curtains and can't figure why it's still here, not out there. But even from the back of the store, Charlie's Volvo—sashaying out onto the empty road (the realtor's "commercially viable major route") and heading south—was easy enough to follow.

Why so early? Iris, the presumed co-fucker, hadn't left with him. She was still in back, making a pre-inventory list of the cartons of components delivered yesterday; Bennett could hear the occasional sandy sound of one box moved against another, not gently. Did Charlie meet someone *else* there? Or could it have something to do with the noises made last week about *buying* the place, the restaurant and motel together? (Thirty thousand each, in two college trusts, had been his mother-in-law's bequest to the girls. Amy *and* Bennett—designated joint money, a stern warning from beyond to watch their steps—were given thirty-six. Whereas Charlie—for years of shit taken, collected, sculpted—was bequeathed a breathtaking, who-could-have-expected-it multi-hundred thousand dollars, the whole extent of which would not be known until Elise's property interests were eventually sold off.)

Or did Charlie just *say* he was going there—to that particular place, that very same motel—for Bennett's ears only? To keep his cuckolded son-in-law perpetually reminded of the terms of penance, of why Bennett came to be looking out of these particular windows to begin with. When he turned away finally Iris stood at the stockroom door, slicking her hairline with her wrist.

"Notice a packing list attached to those ReZonics, the 760s?" She wore one of her bulky homemade sweaters, a gray one today (how could she *not* be warm?). "And what about the box for the Lancisi equalizer—see anything on that? Because I don't."

After he shrugged, she began walking back to stock—but Bennett couldn't wait any longer to know:

"Leaving early tonight?"

She didn't break stride. "No, are you?"

"Not that I know of."

One day three months ago, before Bennett had hung up his coat for the afternoon, Charlie was pulling him into the soundroom, saying, "Everything's tuned." The comparator console was on and each speaker on the carpeted shelves of the glass-enclosed room was alive with purply loud rock music.

"THE NICE THING ABOUT RADIO," Charlie went on, "IS THAT YOU'RE IMMEDIATELY IN THE STREAM. WHAT ELSE CAN YOU ALWAYS SAMPLE FROM THE MIDDLE?"

Bennett found a place for himself against a stationary cabinet of pre-amps. He blew his nose. More vacuuming needed in here, where dust held but sound invariably bled, running into the rest of the cavernous store. How Sid and Charlie had ever been talked into this crude huge space—originally a Robert Hall store, suits on pipe-racks, low running tables of bargain slacks—Bennett couldn't fathom. After Hall's left, a discount/warehouse-priced/second-quality leather-jackets outlet went in; and after that the For Rent sign didn't come down for a good year and a half. As hard as Charlie tried to fiddle with the space, the permanent impression it left was of a store short on goods. The rear sales counter had some density—two display cases of earphones and tapes and disc washers—but the rest was a wilderness, a mouth open to devour them all. The radio music had stopped and a female voice succeeded:

"*Superrrrb.*" (Out of twenty sets of speakers the word was like struck crystal: buzzing, furred). "*Wasn't that nice! 'Elena, Now' and it was by New Improved Zeal, who're, it says here, new out of Boston. We'll go back and take a few more tastes of that later on this afternoon. It's one-eleven on RVW, and somewhere around here I have some facts for you . . .*

"*Okay, here they are: It's currently fifty-seven degrees in the mid-Hudson Valley and eastern Catskills. The wind, according to this, is at six miles an hour, gusting to ten; and the barometer is steady at thirty point oh three. For tonight the forecast is temperatures going down to the mid-thirties up here in the hills but higher, in the forties, down in the valley. Chance of an early morning shower tomorrow, but then clearing and getting milder. Does not say anything here about serious rain or that other dread stuff on into the weekend. If it rains—blame me.*

"*More music now—no, wait, first this: A question I have to ask you about how your room is working. You knew that rooms 'work'? Of course you did. For instance, if right now I sound like a bass-drum or if I'm shrieking like a loon—two possibilities. It could be the fault of your room, and you're going to have to call a contractor, have him rush right over and begin tearing down walls, raising or lowering ceilings . . . Or—you can get yourself down to Route 11 in Tortenville and check out the Sound Barn/Charles Shapes Limited.*"

Charlie, ignoring the common injury to his name, *shapes* instead of *shappis*, grinned excitedly and clutched a shelf's edge.

"*Charles Shapes knows that the ordinary stereo store tries to sell you what they've got priced to move, what the manufacturer has let them have a deal on. Which is okay—except that by the time you the customer enters the process, the bargain's really already in someone else's pocket. What Charles Shapes will explain to you when you go over and talk to him in Tortenville is that it may not pay for you to take that chance immediately. Although his Sound Barn has for sale all the most up-to-date equipment, strictly state-of-the-art, he'll tell you that even if you take home a thousand-dollar set-up, and put it together, then find that it doesn't perform all that well in your particular space—well, you've got a big,* permanent *problem."*

"All the clichés," said Bennett. "Except 'state-of-the-art.' "

"You don't listen. She said it. Shhhh!"

"*—standard policy: Don't like it, bring it back within seven days for a full refund. But seven days isn't a very long time. Good sound equipment has to* mold *to a room, and sometimes there have to be adjustments. Charles Shapes and his experts at The Sound Barn recognize this, and here's how they're unique in this area:—*"

The length of the ad surprised Bennett, considering that Charlie hesitated even to run a mingy few lines in the local *Pennysaver*. "Is she ad-libbing?"

"*. . . five and six and seven months later—whenever it is that the lease runs out—you bring the equipment back, that simple. But say that instead—as probably is going to be the case—you find that there's been love at first listen. In that case, Charles Shapes will deduct your rental payments and sell you your system outright at a price you'll be very happy with. Your system, the one you've already lived with, gotten to know.*"

Bennett stared into space, his chin sunk into a cupped palm. Charlie had better appreciate middles—he *was* one. The rent-to-own policy (which so far had appealed to thankfully few customers) wasn't because Charlie was a shylock. He just couldn't bear to take someone else's money once and for all.

"*So don't put it off any longer. The Sound Barn/Charles Shapes Limited. Route 11, in the Tortenville Plaza, a mile south of the A & P. Go. It's* the *place for tailored sound."*

Charlie turned off the speakers when music followed. "We talked and she took notes, but there was nothing like a script. It's a small station. Well?"

"I'd be on the safe side—"

"Big surprise."

"How much, if I can ask, *is* it costing you?" he said to Charlie.

"The potassium in bananas they say is good for leg cramps. Run over to the A & P."

"I'm fine."

"Eventually I'm sure I'll pay. For now it's costing me zip, nothing. The station owner wants to get me interested in some kind of ministers' group, a church. If I can find it I'll show you the brochure he left. Quite a character. Monte Vogelsang—but calls himself Monte Vee, and the restaurant he owns up in East Dorchester is called Vee's. He also owns a vitamin wholesaling operation, a cheese store, and this radio station. Sid runs across him a lot at civic things but doesn't care for him. Of course who doesn't make Sidney nervous. This church, though, is apparently sort of dubious. A tax dodge. It ordains small businessmen."

Bennett continued rubbing at his leg. "Fine."

"The announcer just now is one of his *Vee-girls*," Charlie continued. "In the Sixties he was a rock-music promoter—he managed that group, you know the name, very famous, up in Woodstock . . . It doesn't come to you either? These rock fellows—"

"*Fine.*"

"—had all these groupies living nearby them. The women got older, children were born, they stayed in the area—and eventually they became employees in Monte Vee's various businesses. Unusual, no?"

Two weeks later, as Bennett walked in for the day at twelve thirty, a woman stood behind the store's rear counter. After a quick exchange of looks with Charlie, she came around, smiling. "I had to make sure you weren't a customer." (Charlie, hanging back, said, "Here it comes—he's going to say *What's a customer?*") She said, "Bennett? Bennett . . . *Shapes?*"—having learned by then to say it correctly.

"Hoooo!" went Charlie. But Bennett was severe: "*Wyler.*"

"Right, I'm sorry—the son-in-*law*. Bennett *Wyler*." A look to Charlie fetching no immediate aid, she turned back: "I'm Iris."

Entertained enough, Charlie left the register. "This is Iris Seavy—did you recognize the voice from the radio? Say yes."

A redhead: that weird complexion. Narrow-faced and thin in a turtleneck and skirt, noticeably big breasts. When Bennett parked his jacket on the halltree in the office he saw a large orange-and-red woven sack in addition to an extravagantly bulky sweater already hanging there. These told him all he needed to know. When he re-emerged, Charlie had gone outside to sweep the sidewalk and the woman already was quietly rounding the floor making notes for herself in the margins of various manufacturers' brochures.

Of the five potential customers in the store that first afternoon, two left with outright purchases. Four more the next day, with the woman—*Iris*—closing on half of them. A man Bennett's age wearing a Western shirt, old corduroys, and a ponytail spent a lot of knowledgeable-looking time examining the various features of different turntables—and Iris had moved in on him eventually to go head-to-head about S/N ratios, load characteristics, tracing holds, impressive technical details.

Yet just as the ponytail's nods were growing deepest, most convinced, the Iris-person (to Bennett's delight) seemed to screw it up completely. Seconds from a sale, she touched one studded cuff of the man's Western shirt and asked him, "Please don't say yes yet." The ponytail squinted. "First bring Kathy down to hear it." The man looked at Iris some more. Then, with a sinking heart, Bennett watched the customer draw cash out of a tooled leather pouch riding his hip, insistent on paying for that particular turntable right there and then. Charlie, like Bennett, had observed from various discreet locations on the floor, disappearing afterwards without a word into the back.

Iris was setting the sales-slip carbons under the register drawer when Bennett approached her, casually filing at a nostril. "Know him?"

"Hawk you mean? He builds looms in Saugerties. Good ones: I have two."

"A friend," Bennett concluded.

"A big fool," she smiled, "in his own way."

"That pouch."

"Why? Did you get a really good look at it up close? They're beautiful, those pouches. A friend of mine makes them."

"The Woodstocks" became Charlie's benign name for this type of customer, more and more of whom came to the Barn, buying mostly smaller portable items, but at least buying something. Iris carried batteries in the pocket of a linen apron she'd taken to wearing around the store like a British nursing sister. She claimed, according to Charlie, never to have sold stereo before. She was a craftsperson and a therapist. The radio-announcer job had been only a temporary fill-in favor to Monte Vee when his afternoon man left suddenly. Bennett understood too from Charlie that she was divorced from a member of Monte's former rock band and had a child who attended some kind of special school. A boy? A girl? Bennett would have liked to know, but Charlie said he didn't have specifics.

Iris was back again from stock, disturbing papers that lay near the register. "Well, I can't find them anywhere. The second time invoices are missing from the same trucker. I give up."

Bennett, who'd been waiting for this—for her excuse to leave, to go join Charlie at the motel—tried casually to delay her. "Is it Beller?"

"He takes advantage of Charles. That we're a little out of the way. It's pique."

"A *lot* out of the way."

"The way of what? A road's a road—he can get here if he wants. Charles maybe is . . . *inconvenient*, but big deal."

Bennett had expected *too nice* instead. The universal opinion. But by now—after hours in a bed in the D-Lux Motel or in Charlie's bed in Goshen or in hers (wherever that was; she was vague about where she came to work from every day); or on the floor of the office, or in her car (Charlie's Volvo probably wouldn't accommodate)—wherever it was that they rested after their frantic digging transactions—by now, if she had anything on the ball at all, she must have begun to realize the truth. Not only Charlie's *not*-niceness but his veritable badness, his pleasure in cruel toying. Which she probably savored (Bennett was positive they were fucking), laughing along with Charlie at him, at Bennett: *A toddler. Unconscious. Needs supervision.*

The real reason why the trucker screws Charlie? Because Charlie *lets* him—knowing eventually it will stop. Never complain and soon enough the trucker will be scrupulous about providing every invoice, bringing every delivery as ordered, making the Sound Barn the first of his stops, never late a day or short a piece—for how could he have ever behaved this way to gentle Charlie Shapes, that nice man with the monstrous patient trust in everyone else's crippling second thoughts?

Iris said, "I'm going to speak to him about considering a change. You should too."

Bennett said, "Change of what?"

Iris frowned at him: "Truckers"—and went back immediately to stock.

Before Iris arrived on the scene, in fact immediately before Bennett himself came to work at the Barn part-time, his wife, Amy, had made a confession. The moment she chose to unburden herself was a few hours after the end of a party, once Bennett had returned from driving the babysitter home. (A strangely exalting ride: a sweatiness to the road lights and Bennett's tipsy respect for the mystery of the car's mechanics—how this beat-up, maligned Toyota of Amy's maintained speed and smoothness, an uncomplaining partner at every turn, posting and stretching, going too fast yet gliding to a squeal-less stop in front of Kerry's parents' split-level. Even a hint—from the way she sat there in the car a moment longer than necessary—that Kerry might naughtily be thinking about kissing him, grinding her teensy breasts against his chest.) In the kitchen, he found Amy sitting at the dinette table, faced in the direction of the sink.

"Look at all of them, Benny. Just look." Pots and casseroles full of sullen dead suds crowded the stovetop and the sink; back-to-back parties, two in as many days—the Wylers hosting Friday's, Saturday night's at the Collards—had been the good-at-the-time idea of the three depressed friends: Amy, Ruth Collard, and Theresa Dellamatraccia. "Benny" being a reliable sign she'd had more to drink than he had (though he'd had a fair amount himself), Bennett dropped himself down beside her and took her hand.

Amy said, "What are we going to *do*?"

"About what?"

"About *those*."

Bennett got up to step toward the sink—clapping hands (Amy once complained that very little he did annoyed her quite as much as his overly loud hand claps) and feeling himself squeezed by a spasm of love for domestic life, something which right then seemed scaled down to perfect size: a matter of getting places at night in cars, of easily mollifying a drunken wife, of uncomplicated pots addressable with equally uncomplicated hot soapy water.

"We'll never do this again," Amy swore. Bennett wrenched the taps. "And in case I puke . . ."—right behind him now, looking into the cabinet above Bennett's right ear—". . . I guess this green Tupperware one . . ."

She returned unsteadily to the table, holding the plastic bowl.

"Don't blame me, you know," she said, "for not doing those today. I told you why. I was getting the oaktag for the Parents' Association. Ours was better, you know."

"The food for sure."

"The whole party."

Bennett decided to pull on the pink Playtex gloves draped across the faucet. "And Theresa couldn't stand it. Here, everyone had fun spontaneously."

"She was telling me last week that she wants to live on a boat someday and have endless parties. Her romantic fantasy."

"Silly girl." Since under the best of circumstances Bennett had trouble with the words *woman* or *man* (which he understood to signify the stage prior to the *dying* of any particular girl or boy), now—tipsy, full of loving pity for Amy the dying ex-girl and himself the dying ex-boy—the words would have been abhorrent, and he swung around to look at his wife with fatty love. She was staring dully at the ball-fringed valence above the sink window, the Tupperware bowl ovaled between her knees.

"Theresa is my rival, I hope you realize. She is. We compete."

Bennett turned back to the dishes. Half the first casserole had wiped out nicely, but the rest resisted. Traces of the from-scratch sauce they'd served with the manicotti tinted the sink's stainless steel. Hot as it was, the soapy water of itself wasn't enough for the job.

"If I wanted to, I would really be able to do something extremely bad to her. Something *extremely* bad. Like murder her."

"At least."

"You'd like to see her dead also, right?"

"Is there Brillo here somewhere?" Bennett put one knee down before the cabinet under the sink. "This here, is this ammonia?"

"If I did kill her one day, you know what people would think. Keep this in mind. They'd think you were having an affair with her and I found out. Or that you knew that I was about to find out, so *you* killed her to shut her up—and have me blamed."

"Sounds better." Uncapped, the ammonia in vain tried to smell fruity.

"Because you may not know this, but she does have lovers."

Pouring some of the liquid directly into the sink, some onto a Dobie Pad, Bennett said, "Well, I never told you *this* before, but . . ." Amy, even high, didn't find this kind of thing funny. There was a jellied silence. Suds were bunched on the rubber gloves, so Bennett turned carefully to her. "I am *not* having an affair with our pal Mrs. Gimme-I-Wannit-All-a."

Amy was looking down at her feet. "She's my *rival*, I told you. She does what I do."

"And *your* current heavy fling?" The gloves were dripping onto his shoes; Bennett was forced to face the sink again.

Amy gave a small, dry cough. Taking it as the start of a laugh, Bennett smiled. Another cough jumbled and expanded, becoming a semi-retch—and Amy covered her eyes with her palms, fingers splayed above her hair like the tines of a crown.

Bennett squeezed the Dobie Pad in horror. "I don't want to know." (This strained, mangled peep was his voice? It was.) And just as daintily, ridiculously: "I mean that. I *don't*."

Was it very warm in the room? Amy was crying now, and Bennett had to command himself *Don't*—then was surprised how quickly the instinct to walk over and comfort her was checked.

So this is happening to me. And I seem to know what to do—feeling stretched, *neat*, all of a dry piece, a nine-year-old again, wholly selfish, without fear of a penalty.

Her hands came away from her eyes for a moment. "With—" she

began, but Bennett, wincing, shot up a pink rubber hand, eyes drilling desperately into the Mexican raffia donkeycart on the window ledge above the sink. At that moment he was struck, and hard, by something that caught him on the lower spine. It felt like a baseball.

"You threw *vomit* at me?"—the Tupperware bowl rocking at his feet as he beat at the back of his pants (though clearly the bowl was empty). The bitch, he'd kill her!

In the meantime Amy took the opportunity to quietly insert the name: "Merrit."

Bennett kicked the bowl, bent and retrieved it, slammed it down upon the counter, the poor noise it made at last reminding him that silence and not shouting usually was to his advantage when they fought. "Fine," he said. His nose was numb.

"You're *letting* me?" Amy gave a surprisingly bitter sob. "I knew it!"

"Absolutely corright you are." The nose-numbness had spread downward to affect his lips, his tongue. "I am."

Amy cried, "Shitshit! *Go right ahead? Be my guest?* You're that cruel?"

His limpness gored her? He'd slow it down by half again. "Looks like it."

"You hate me *that* much?"

"You poor poor thing." Where the bowl hit, Bennett's spine ached; he rubbed patronizingly at the knobs there, staring at the wet serving dishes. Merrit Heubsch. Pale stringy Merrit! Once when weather hadn't allowed the quartet to fly to Montreal for a booking at McGill, and a train was taken instead (hours edging endless Lake Champlain, snow dropping into the water), Bennett had observed Merrit the Silverfish yank two small, foil-wrapped packages from the side pocket of his jacket: a pair of tiny apples in one, a paperweight-sized chunk of white cheese in the other. With a pocketknife unclipped from his keychain, he proceeded to cut narrow slices of first one and then the other apple. Bennett, offered, refused any—after which Merrit went on to peel each separate section until only fuzzes of pulp still attached to the parings. And then ate manicured apple followed by exquisite cube of cheese. Hypnotized unwillingly, Bennett had never seen a human appetite satisfied this bloodlessly . . . and of course now knew that Merrit Heubsch also *fucked* this way exactly, with clean sinew and up on outstretched arms, with an unnotching rhythm upon Amy's opened body (was Amy even pretty enough? *clean* enough?)—as with a thud, adultery now began to make Bennett feel truly sick. As though he himself had been screwed—screwed not so much by Merrit *as by comparison itself*. He and Merrit even wore the same green Irish tweed hat!

When he grabbed at one of the slippery casseroles—to smash it to the floor (*Now I'll never be able to wear that goddamn green hat again!*)—Bennett was unable to haul it from the suds and had to settle instead for saying the name back at Amy in an ambassadorial way until—by the third repetition—it started losing strong connection with the first violinist's actual person.

Amy waited him out. Revived and defiant, she announced dryly: "I exercised a privilege. My free will. What do I have it for if I'm never going to use it? I'm very sorry now and I hate to hurt you—but at the time I *had* to."

"Why don't you shout a little louder, so your daughters are sure to hear this swell little piece of sickness?" Bennett himself had forgotten till now that the girls were in the house. "So they can be brought up too, like you were, to look at life as a bunch of *privileges* to be exercised."

Amy rose, looking shocked. Quickly Bennett walked away (in case she was going for something to hit him, kill him with) and into the half-bathroom off the garage, where he locked the door behind him.

"He *told* you?" Amy cried in.

Bennett's, in the mirror, was a face unprepared for life. Down now to a whisper, Amy's voice still was carrying: "My father *knows*. He saw me. Going to a mote . . . to a place. But he never brings it up—and I can't take it anymore!"

Bennett removed his wedding band, slipping it onto his key ring. And although he didn't feel his eyes were quite hard enough to pull it off completely, he picked up the ceramic toothbrush cup and let it drop to the floor. (Footsteps from Marcie's room overhead quickened at the shatter.) "*Saw you?*" he bellowed through the door. "How'd you manage *that?*"—one more time ashamed by Amy's ineptitude, Amy who couldn't fry an egg that didn't burn, who couldn't manage a mixed deposit at the bank, who didn't know how to switch on the tape deck or make a decent U-turn.

He opened the door when for a long while there wasn't an answer. The floorboards went on creasing and sighing overhead, but no one was in sight. The dimensions of the mess began to go tricky on him, all alone (*Because I smashed a cup?*) and in a moment he feared he'd be the one who was apologetic first. Before that terrible thing could happen, he took his coat and stepped quietly out to the garage and drove to his office in the Rabbit.

The arts consortium leased space in an old Victorian Poughkeepsie building—gingerbread fronting, mullioned windows, some graffiti markered on at street level—just a block from the riverfront. But two nights of sleeping there turned out to be all he could stand. When the Unitarian counseling service on the first floor let out its last group session of the evening, there were the sounds of troubled people: individual feet approaching individual cars, ignitions. And in the morning he woke too early, lifting his shoulders against the weakly glued arm of the sofa, seeing the dawn river build toward color through the westernmost window. The office was no refuge. He used to hustle to book concerts for the quartet featuring you-know-who at this very desk. Nor did Amy call—and what if she never did?

Also—if he *didn't* go home, he'd have to buy himself new

clothes: a fresh shirt, new underwear, change of socks. High emotion was one thing, shopping another—Bennett being in all things, bad or good, the sort of man who actually desired only what he already had. He began envisioning a plausible return: Amy abjectly sorry about Merrit, Bennett in return crisply regretting he'd smashed the toothbrush cup.

He went home unannounced—and found no girls, no Amy, no Toyota in the garage. No note. Only the phone ringing.

At a diner right off the Thruway exit near the store, he met Charlie as summoned (and on the telephone Charlie had given nothing away, made believe he knew nothing was wrong). Charlie read the menu and did all the talking. "Halibut. Scrod. Bluefish. Swordfish. Sole. Flounder. *Sea trout!* for God's sakes, red snapper—you're supposed to believe this'll all be fresh?" while Bennett chose merely to have a cup of Brim. "I need you to come in with me, help me out a little. José you know quit . . . No more than three afternoons a week—a promise . . . You can still do whatever else you have to do in the mornings. Times like these family turns to family—the only ones you can trust . . . All I have to do is just *seem*, Bennett, to be about breaking even—and then Telscher will be off my back. Such a pain you don't know. A rider, a leaner. It's his boredom, but I don't know how long I'm going to be able to stand it."

Bennett himself had no friends (he had women instead: his wife, his daughters) and he distrusted the whole idea of friendship—but even someone like Bennett knew that if there was such a thing as a true friend, who didn't ride, didn't lean, it was Sid Telscher. Almost a brother to Charlie, neighbors first in various sections of Brooklyn, now Goshen. Twenty-eight years together selling pianos. Telscher grew rich: investments in Laundromat franchises, shopping centers, while Charlie stayed relatively poor, most of what he earned put to securing college for Amy, for a Bechstein grand, for concert and opera subscriptions, for his record collection and ultra-safe cars. But Sid was always there for Charlie, had stood by his decision to sell to the Jamaicans, the Goolsbys, had capitalized the audio store (guilty, Bennett's guess, at having sold the piano business out from under Charlie); now hadn't made even a peep of protest about the innocently asinine rental-policy idea. The irritant was not Sid Telscher, no. Bennett knew what—who—the irritant was.

"At the moment you happen to have the time . . . You'll audition a new cellist, I know . . ." (Here it came.) ". . . but believe me because I know—thirty-five years of listening to serious music, after all—chamber-music groups like these are delicate mechanisms. The right person isn't found that quickly. In any case, this job working for me would be strictly very temporary." (The toying, the feinting—so unnecessary. Bennett in his wrinkled shirt, who'd gone to Poughkeepsie to sulk but returned two days later when his socks ripened. Why hadn't Charlie just lowered the boom and gotten it over with?) "Only afternoons and only until you get a new cellist and I get a new manager to replace José. All right, I've said what *I* have to say. Your turn now. Speak. Say no."

"And you know what else?"—pointing with a forkful of nesselrode pie. "We'll be closer, all of us. I think we'll have fun."

Charlie's notion of fun, though . . .

Fun like the advent of Iris? Fun like Amy's subsequent hopelessness and irritability since promising (under fatherly pressure, Bennett was sure) that she was done with *him* (Merrit had no name anymore to either of them), that it was permanently broken off? Fun like—most recently, in April—Florida? Charlie had insisted on making his own flight arrangements, leaving Bennett, Amy, and the girls down there alone most of the first day, waiting at Elise's friends' apartment down the hall. They were faced with platters of fish, rolls, cream cheese, butter, sliced Swiss and Munster and a dish of scallions, tomatoes, and cucumbers; juices, an automatic Bunn machine spitting out pot after pot of piney-smelling coffee; Amy, more tired than grieving, ate, as did the girls, while Bennett closeted himself in the bedroom with Harry Schiffman.

Fun? Opening Elise's envelope—INSTRUCTIONS—had made Bennett feel like he was sticking ungloved fingers into the woman's dead mouth. Harry's wife Mickey (thin and that dark Chinese-sparerib sun-worshipper color) slipped in to join them. "Keep in mind what a dignified woman she was basically. And with reason. To have made a new life down here for herself, made new friends, built her business up so successfully—*and* to be social on top of it all! It would have been much easier to hide in that house in Brooklyn the rest of her life and never show her face, and for all intents and purposes be dead. But she didn't. Now you tell me, that's not worth something? Worth letting her have this last thing, whatever you or Harry or me or any of us think of it?"

"To Whom It May Concern" (a deckled page, blue sateen finish to the underside of the envelope—the identical semi-formal stationery the Wylers owned, courtesy of Elise: a tenant of hers a stationer). "In the event of my passing away, I ask that these steps are taken quickly: Notified should be my daughter Amy Shapes Wyler"—the phone number, complete with area code—"and either Mr. or Mrs. Harry Schiffman"—the number—"after which arrangements for cremation WITHOUT A SERVICE should be made as quickly as possible. No service should be connected either with the disposal of the ashes, which I hereby instruct and demand should be scattered into the sea, brought there by boat. Mr. and Mrs. Schiffman, should they succeed me, will know how to make arrangements for this." It was signed and bore a notary's stamp.

Dignity? An enormous *grudge* was more like it, big as the size of her. Calculation, selfishness, exploitation of her family's weakness. The letter rankled Bennett. Self-righteous, smug little people though they were, his own parents were the ones with dignity. Called in Sun City last night, his father tried to sound shocked, while his mother didn't fumble for a second about whether they'd fly in from Arizona for the funeral: "Is Amy in any shape to talk? Then give her kisses from us and our deepest condolences. We'll speak to you when you get home. Call us, dear, won't you?" None of this obese living and sudden dying, these surprise documents, for them.

While he read INSTRUCTIONS, his younger daughter Marcie was killing a seagull. The sound of her sister Betsa's half-scared, half-thrilled voice ("*Yeeiiii!*" then a long, burning intake of air around clenched teeth, "*Eeeessshhhhhhh*") preceded the sound of running steps, a slammed door, Amy's voice ("*Shit*, Betsa!"), and an aggrieved response ("*Me?* Oh sure! everyone blame me, come on—I'm the one who's in the bathroom now, who slammed the stupid door, I'm the one who killed the stupid bird!"). Marcie had brained it with a tomato pitched whole over the side of the terrace. Minutes later, as he stood at the railing looking down, spangles of light snagged on Bennett's eyebrows, weighing the lids so that for a moment he only saw in black and white the image of the big bird-body, dirty with tomato goo, flat on the sand seven stories below. Harry Schiffman already had rushed down and was in view now, striding out of the building's beachside entrance. In time he had company—a woman in a red and yellow housecoat who later returned upstairs with Harry and turned out to be the only one with any success at coaxing Marcie out of the bathroom.

"Honeybunch, this is Mrs. Gutterman, from the building. I'm on my terrace so I was able to see it come down right before my eyes and then what. The little thing got stunned was all that happened, I went down to check. It rested for a minute and then got up, flew away."

(In the living room Amy turned away: "Great. Lie to her. That's great." Bennett hissed at her to be still.)

"I'm right there on four, I see it all the time: if the water's bad they sit and float, but sometimes there are tremendous waves and they look like they're hurt. They're not. They shake themselves good and they fly away, goodbye! Not that you should expect it to come back to the exact same place. It learned a lesson, getting too close to a building. Like you learned a lesson too—am I right, honeybunch?"

Later that afternoon, the girls gone shell hunting with Mickey and Harry, Bennett accompanied Amy in Harry's car to the docks—to find the *Blue Marie*, the boat the funeral parlor referred them to. The captain, Captain Molinaro, brought them below to look at a rack of cassettes, should they desire music. The "scatterings," they were told, were twice a week—anytime from five onward, and Thursdays were best. But Charlie was there at last by the time they returned, taking belated charge, okaying cremation (the grotesquely large casket would be no better) but no ash scattering. Instead two teak boxes of the ashes were eventually carried home on the Delta jet—plus, on Amy's insistence (after an argument with her father), one box of Elise's enormous clothing.

Fun like that?

Iris was now up front for keeps, beginning the receipts, and Bennett stood rubbing the glass of the already polished counter. For a long time they didn't speak.

"Know what I've noticed?" Iris recounted some stiff new bills. "You don't have your own demonstrators here. Charles has his trusty Polonaises and Sibelius and *The Planets* and I've got my Clapton and the Orff, but you just put on FM or borrow ours. Someone could get the idea—even with the kind of jobs you have, this one and your other—that you're not all that gung-ho about music in the first place."

"And someone"—Bennett gave an insincere smile—"would be wrong."

"Taking music or leaving it: you think that's terrible, don't you."

Bennett recalled Charlie saying she was divorced from a musician. "You're the former disc jockey, not me." The charge slips, stacked in an open-topped box, today were, almost every one of them, her sales—yet Bennett reserved the right to tally them and he reached across her arms.

"Well, I don't have the same problems with it. Maybe if I knew how to *make* music, produce it—but I don't, and what I'd make is just sounds. So I face it: all I am of music is a consumer." She ironed a single with the side of one hand. "That's not the attitude you're *supposed* to have, I realize. You're supposed to feel more spiritual, you're supposed to *love* music. I like breathing the fresh air when I leave here after work—but does that mean I *love* fresh air? When it comes my way I welcome it."

The tissue of the charge slips was greasy. "Your lungs," Bennett said, "a lot more than *welcome* fresh air."

"You know musicians personally—"

He looked carefully at her.

"—so you know how up-front they are. They don't romanticize it like that. They know it's only disturbed air, that happens to stimulate certain nerves. It's *pleasant*, absolutely, to have those particular nerves stimulated—but *love*? People turn into music *lovers* and feel they have to go into this death pact with it?"

Bennett leaned across her for the scratch-pad beside the register—

"No comment," Iris concluded. "Music is art, right? It uplifts the *soul*?"

—and in the leaning his elbow accidentally made weak contact with one of her breasts under sweater and shirt. "Music is music. This"—he waved the pad close to her nose—"is disturbed air."

"Ooh, angry." She drew the pad from his grip. "We're only having a *conversation*, remember. Charles, to give you an example, makes believe he isn't into accumulation. But watch him when a record he likes is on: he rakes it in. People's faces are the same way listening to music as when they count money. You recognize what I'm saying is true, but it's inconvenient for you."

Bennett said nothing and began adding the charge amounts with a pencil on the back of a piece of register tape, forsaking the calculator at the other side of her.

"You're a little offended? Don't be. Think of all the unknowables.

Whatever it is that's making me enjoy provoking you, but also is making you be so extra-touchy. And let it go at that." Recounting the cash, Iris started humming Chopin.

She was crazy. Divorced-from-a-musician crazy. But she had a point. He ought to try and view her craziness as amusing—it was the best, the easiest approach. Bennett knelt when a twenty slipped off the countertop, finding it stopped against the tan heel of one of her shoes. Already one of her hands had dropped down, her forefingers walking in the air, nearly brushing his nose as they asked for the bill back.

"If I went to someone's house to watch television, and the program was so offensive to me that I stood up and shut off the set—*maybe* that would be tolerated." She snapped a rubber band around a stack of singles. "You agree? The hosts wouldn't necessarily like it, but they'd probably understand. Do you think I could get away with the same thing if we were listening to a symphony?"

(Had he been *expected* to dive for the bill? A distinctly fruity odor had pulsed from her stockings or legs.)

Lights all of a sudden were swinging through the store—a car's headlamps, poking into the front windows like sword tips. A customer this late wasn't usual. Was it Charlie, coming back for her? But in the time it took Bennett to walk to the windows the car had turned away. "Probably police," Iris said—"checking." Red taillights (not Volvo-shaped) were loitering at the exit to the lot before dimming out. The car was simply sitting there next to the sign stanchion. "Is someone picking you up?" Bennett asked her.

Coming up behind him, Iris moved him over an inch, her fingers light on his waist. "In East Dorchester they patrol the merchants in unmarked cars."

"Well, by standing here we're advertising there are only two of us." Bennett pulled at her arm, but instead Iris went forward—she opened the door and was out.

Crazy could also *not* be amusing. (Charlie's expression when he finds us shot in the head, lying in pools of blood . . .) His heart whining, Bennett returned to the back counter, where he squared the piles of money and charge slips by the cash register, shoving them into plainer view. Iris would be returning as if in a nightmare, with horror in tow, a gun or two at her back, and he wanted the gunmen to have no trouble seeing that everything was right here waiting for them, no need to hunt or murder for it.

However Iris returned alone—stopping first to check her watch, then locking the front door from the inside. "Some poor guy lost, totally wrong side of the river, looking for Cold Spring." Idly she moved the money that was leaning half on and half off the counter's far edge. She reached under the register for the night-deposit bag.

"Couldn't he have come in to ask directions?" Bennett wanted to know.

"What about folk art?" she said, out of the blue. "Familiar with it? Wonderful stuff. My brother's a dealer and our house is full of it. In fact there's a museum exhibition opening soon that we should go down to with our kids . . ." She was stuffing cash as well as two personal checks and the credit-card slips into the deposit sack. "Whenever you're ready, I'll lock up behind you."

"Aren't you leaving?"

"It has to be my error—missing those two invoices somewhere. If I don't try to find them at least once more . . ."

Bennett pulled the money bag away from her. "I'll drop this off then at the bank."

"I can do it—I'm a big girl." She studied him humorously. "The expression on your face when I came back in! Did you think we were being robbed?"

"Robbed?" Bennett laughed. The bag in hand, he went for his windbreaker in Charlie's office. "*Robbed?*"

3

Smiled-at and smiling back in the antechamber following the regular Saturday morning service, Shapes drank a shot of blended whiskey from a Dixie cup and watched Telscher at the far side of the synagogue foyer trading magazines and subscription newspapers with a knot of other men.

Shapes had said not only the mourner's Kaddish for Elise but Torah blessings as well—called on as an honor, being the town's next auditor's best buddy and business associate. The cantor cantillated, the silver scroll-plate of the auxiliary Torah tinkled an intermittent music, and looking in at the opened Ark (the still other scrolls leaning in sumptuous velvets—all dressed up, nowhere to go), Shapes felt there might be an opportunity here, if he could just nudge it along, for one of his experiences, what he thought of as his "peelings-back." The first one, years ago, had come on a Yom

Kippur—and although after that they pretty much happened anywhere and anytime, he liked to think the kernel was religious. Having inexplicable interior experiences was as embarrassing to him as to anyone, and to think there was something sacred about them helped.

Yet open as he was to it today—gazing at the Ark, returning with concentration to the scroll of parchment resting on the lectern: the mitered edges and saclike widths of the letters—nothing happened. The peelings-back, the openings-up, they asked for patience, and he was willing to give it some time—but finally the sexton, standing at the *bima* to his right, had had to nudge him ("You're done") to sing the closing blessing.

After the whiskey Shapes chose a miniature Danish, which he then choked on a little as the dry dab of cheese cut off his air, his ears singing a high pearly note. The sounds of Shapes's cough were what drew Sid away from his friends.

"Wrong pipe?" There was a roll of printed matter under his arm. "Do you believe this nudnik Pesseroff still subscribes to Russian-language journals? Though I'm not complaining. Some I'll take home and some we'll give to our friend." The synagogue had received a letter written by a local ex-convict, a Soviet Jew currently living in the area, who was seeking, as Shapes understood it, no more than a bit of fellow-feeling from brother Jews, a warm and forgiving hand. In the letter, the man had made brief mention of a "temper"—but the idea of a proudly free-swinging Soviet Jew only appealed that much more to Sidney, who'd been excited for a week about this afternoon's meeting: helping the poor man as you might an endangered species, some overly brawny, but essentially disadvantaged, victim of jungle circumstance. Telscher now glanced at the tray of pastries: "Anything good?"

"Try the cheese," Shapes suggested.

The copies of the magazines in Russian, plus the one in Yiddish, *Sovetish Heymland,* sat on the back seat while Shapes and Telscher drove in Sid's Merce toward Peekskill—stopping on the way, as planned, at a mall and after a short discussion buying a plaid flannelette man's shirt. "Medium?" "Safest." "Gift-wrap it?" "To celebrate what?" "Just in a bag? Is that *nice?*" While Telscher waited for the salesgirl to locate a box, Shapes browsed through the Photography/Cameras section.

The rest of the ride to Peekskill was Shapes's chance to do what he'd promised himself—bring up the subject of buying Sid out—and yet as Telscher nattered on ("I pulled out my old Russian books last night, the ones from the Workers' School Morty used to drag me to on Saturday mornings. The grammar text and the one on Soviet history . . ."), Shapes kept thinking instead of the Torah lectern and the "peeling-back" experience of that earlier Yom Kippur—Elise, of course, unable and unwilling to fast; bored at noon, worse by one, and nasty by two: flailing remarks about religion and hypocrisy. And since Amy had wanted to be taken to Mikey Telscher's anyway, it was as good a time as any for father and daughter to escape.

Sid and Dorie at the time lived on the top floor of a two-family house, six of them altogether including the boys and Sid's old mameh. Amy went off with Michael to one of the back bedrooms, while the older boys lay on the living room floor between the heavy furniture and legs of the piano to watch the ball game on television; the four adults took the air out on the canted front porch, sliding around on the green-and-white flowered cushions of a worn garden furniture set.

At one point old Mrs. Telscher waddled inside on ankles like navel oranges and returned to offer around a glass dish of salted nuts. "Ma!" Doris was up in a flash, swooping like a falcon, while Sidney eyed his mother with all the oceanic history of being her son. The old lady was another Elise—a dull anger looking for any whetstone. Shapes recalled a long-ago Yom Kippur when, in plain view of Sid's father (no eclair himself: a thin little rake, a gambler) who was standing only yards away talking with cronies on Neptune Avenue, she came down to the stoop—to the mopey famished Morty, Irving, Sidney, and Charles—bringing with her a waxed-paper plate of schmaltz and cut up scallions on thick slices of corn-rye bread.

"Getting a little cool, no?" Sidney's invitation to come inside seemed pointedly to exclude his mother. But in she came too, bringing the dish of nuts. It and the television, the roughhousing boys, the Yankees—any second now Shapes's inevitable holy-day headache was going to descend. Telscher put on Serkin—the *Wanderer Fantasy*—as Amy reappeared with Michael. Both had their jackets on; Mikey was going to walk her home.

"You had my white bean salad lately?" asked old Mrs. Telscher. And: "Your wife?—she goes to *shul?*" before answering her own question: "Nah." Sidney opened two miniatures of Hennessey (the latest doctor's "orders" for a case of Telscher angina never proven to actually exist) as Shapes, paying no attention to Schubert, watched the Yankees finish their heartless winning. David, the eldest boy, rose on his elbows to shut off the set. "Maybe I was watching?" "You were out *there*, Grams!" "*Her nor?*—such a mouth!" Light from the alleyway sieved through the drawn batiste curtains behind the sofa. Shapes had a sip of his brandy, and when the dish on the coffee table became just too irresistible, one salted cashew. The old lady ordered Sidney to change the record, which amazingly he did: "This is Horowitz now, Ma, happy? The human schmaltz machine?" Telscher and Shapes were Schnabelites, admiring as well Gieseking, Serkin, Kraus, Cortot, de Larrocha, Gilels, and Novaes, and only parting ways over Arrau and Rubinstein—Shapes loved Arrau; Rubinstein was solely for Sidney. The old lady picked at her bodice. "You play *besser.*" Shapes got to his feet to go. "See?" Sid accused his mother, "driven away by the treacle." Shapes leaned to kiss the top of her dry-smelling head. She asked the knot of his tie: "*Vuz iz* trickle?" "Pudding—made with beef fat." "I use only My-T-Fine." Doris came out of the kitchen to ask Shapes to stay, but in the same breath said: "Tell Michael, if you see him on the Parkway, I want him home."

"Very sweet," Telscher amplified for his mother. "*Too* sweet—like this piano playing." The old lady waved it away dismissively, turning back to Shapes. "Regards to your wife. She stays all day?"

Except for Dorie's request to waylay Michael, Shapes would have walked the side streets rather than busy Ocean Parkway, four lanes of noisy traffic raking through the middle of the broad boulevard (though less so that day) and a pair of paved strips—one for walkers, one a bridle path—flanking the roadway. They in turn were sided by service roads allowing access to the apartment buildings and private homes. Since Amy wouldn't have walked back on the pedestrian strip (she loved horses and horseshit, fresh or strawcake-dried), Shapes made his way over the cinder-dirt composite, keeping a good pace over the bumps, ruts, and chucks. However, near Avenue J, he hit a section of path—as chewed-up-looking as the rest—that felt unusually smooth underfoot.

There the air seemed to sit slightly cold under the trees; veins of sun warmth running through the branches had weakened. Shapes had the odd impulse to inspect his hands—which turned out to look about what he thought his hands usually looked like, but not exactly. The same thing with his feet: close-enough-looking yet not quite. And which, like his hands, felt vaguely far away—as did, he realized, his chest and ribcage. What was going on? A few sips of cognac? The one cashew on an empty stomach?

His walk was straight, his head was clear—yet now he was starting to feel something even more unusual. That he was *remembering* his entire body. That what was walking down Ocean Parkway was a copy from memory of the original.

I'm dying, he concluded. On Yom Kippur, on a horsepath.

Bearing down in the privacy of his approximately recollected body, Shapes tried to halt the process, stop whatever he was having, heart attack or stroke, right then and there. He brought his chin up sharply, to get it level again with reality before it was too late— which was when, raising his eyes, he saw an Ocean Parkway that had opened out like a cleavered melon, where everything was simultaneously pushing back and jawing wide. The sky itself was jumping higher and broader and distances were vast: if he'd wanted to cross the service road and enter the glass front door of one of the apartment houses, he'd need another lifetime. The surface outlines of things seemed the same, but *stretchier*—everything giving itself more and more inner room, loden-leafed yew bushes becoming unlimited forests, sycamores swaying in breezes reaching them from unthinkable realms of sky, covering miles with each tremble. (In which case this probably *wasn't* dying. Dying probably wouldn't be this open. Maybe this swift, but not so wide.) Buildings behind hedges, lobbies pocketed within buildings, apartments past lobbies, rooms set beyond apartment doors—there was a sense of everything elongating, and Shapes felt the urge to open his arms in frightened greeting to all this awesome clearance. (Yet what if his arms flew off like rockets? The best he managed to do was wriggle his shoulders shyly, as if adjusting his jacket.)

Then the wind diminished, the buildings drew back closer to the sidewalks, the sidewalks to the curbs. The horsepath felt solider, and like underwear Shapes's arms and legs crept back into proportion. By the time he was crossing Foster Avenue, it seemed to be all over.

But what? What was over? What had *happened?* Anything? Hunger? The brandy, the nut? Pale as the faces of the devout fasters returning to the synagogue for more atoning, the backs of Shapes's hands were the only remaining evidence.

At that moment, out of nowhere, Mikey Telscher hove into view running at full tilt. Shapes opened his arms and feinted left. He feinted right. He feinted left, right, left, and Mikey, giggling buoyantly, slid by him like a comet.

The halfway house was a converted YMCA in a not good part of Peekskill. Telscher was even considering a no-parking zone—the car at least would be under *negative* police protection—when Shapes spotted a small lot at the side of the building.

The bearded young man who greeted them at the front office ("For Roitmann?") came back into the shadowed rec room a few minutes later leading a short, broad-chested, fortyish-looking man with thinning brown hair. He wore eyeglasses and janitorially plain clothes, a short-sleeve shirt and slacks.

Sidney stuttered between sitting and standing, but the man quickly took an unfussy place at the wooden card table. Sid began, trying his best to sound comfortable. *"Vus hertz'ich, Vitaly?"*

The man, in English, morosely recommended: "You like to call me Chal."

"Al?" Shapes said.

"Chal"—with mouth opened dentist-wide.

"I'm Sidney Telscher and this is Charlie Shapes."

"You're lawyer?" This visibly confused Sid. The Russian pointed to Shapes: "And also not this man?" His left forearm, Shapes saw, was tattooed: a heart pierced with a thick, banal arrow, crude enough for it to have been an hour old and drawn in Magic Marker. Remarkable too were the Soviet eyeglasses: part industrial goggles, part something you'd see in a novelty store; thick gray translucent frames with metallic diamonds trapped within, like chaser lights around a movie marquee.

"We're from Congregation B'nai Abraham. In Crescent Hill? You wrote a letter to our Men's Club—"

"Don't you *have* a lawyer?" Shapes interrupted Telscher.

"*Shit* is what," and the Russian made a dry explosive *pah* with his lips.

"Not of help to you?"

Contemptuously: "Ligl-aid."

A list occurred to Sidney instantly—"Henry Berson, Jack Komisar . . ."—but Shapes stopped him with a hand, turning back to the Russian. "Your legal status now—what is it?"

"*Panyemayete Russki?*"

Shapes shook his head. Sidney, though, nodded, taking a deep breath, eyes softly petitioning for mercy, for the Russian to go slowly—but Vitaly/Al was already launched into it. Shapes soon received the digest.

"He feels that these legal-aid attorneys are government agents. Information getters. State lackeys."

"Help me *nothing* before," Vitaly/Al amended in English, "and not now too."

"Your family is over here with you?"

The man scrutinized Shapes. "What is *your* job?" To Telscher: "And yours?"

"Charles has a store. He sells stereo—*pray . . . igryyev . . . atyl?* record players? I'm semi-retired."

"Job is something I must have, you understand?"

Shapes admitted to being not altogether clear on what Vitaly's status was. Didn't being in a halfway program mean he already had to be holding a job?

The Russian was incredulous. "Think I live here? Just to get *away* I'm here. Special. And what job? In *cleaners?*"

"We're not really up on all this," Telscher apologized, but Shapes said, "You're working there now, in a cleaners?"

"In Khabarovsk I am a radio technician—electrical engineer from Institute." Significance hung like hardware on his expression. "For your store, *anything* you need I can do. Know a lot. Know a *great* lot."

Telscher set an impressed finger across Shapes's wrist as though chording a guitar. "Khabarovsky. *Siberia.* You somehow don't imagine Jews."

Through a smile, his first and largely of gold, Vitaly/Al said: "Father is graduate of Tarbut gymnasium in Kishinev. Siberia I go when they send me, after my school. But not to like very much: *groy-*

ser kalt and too big, too big. People only are nice. Russia, people nicer than here."

"It's a built-up city, Khabarovsky, no?"

"Write down for me names and addresses and telephones, okay, where you live. Where?"

"Not that far from here," said Sid. "Across the river."

"And you?" Shapes asked. "Before . . . here?"

"Brooklyn, Sheepshead Bay—know this?"

"*Landsmen* nearly!" exclaimed Sid, but Shapes modified: "*Were*. Are you familiar with Midwood Park?"

The Russian assured them "Midwood shits" but balanced it with a compliment for Sidney: "You know much of Soviet Union, huh?"

Just then Shapes's ears (set off like an alarm by talk of Midwood?) began to rumble with a wowing metallic note. Telscher waded again into a stream of rusty Russian, happily buttered up by complimentary "*Harashaw! harashaw!*"s, but Shapes's head-noise had turned him impatient:

"Vit . . . Al. We don't know *much* about why you're here."

"Read file?" Shapes said he hadn't. "The ligl-aid then—he tell you a lot of shit? HIAS? Child Services?" Shoulders collared up behind him, the Russian's hands left the card table to drop between his knees. "I tell you then, okay?"

"Okay."

To Sid: "Okay?"

"Okay."

"I drive taxi when we first come here from Israel—"

"You lived in Israel?" said Telscher. "Where?"

"Not good. Beersheva. Not very good for us."

"Drove a taxi . . ." Shapes led him back.

"At Kennedy—on line—in front of International Arrivals building where always we stay. This Puerto Rican fuck . . . *out* of line swings . . . and like that! takes fare from me. So, later, I see him again, near Van Wyck? He yells something to me, I yell back him—you know how it is, right? I pull to the side, he pull to the side; he gets his, you know, tire iron? and out of cab he comes. Is thinking, you know: I'm Russian, I'm *evrei*, *zhidh*, can push around. I have big lead pipe too I find once in Herald Square? I take it out. Know what I mean? Know how I'm saying?"

Later on, in the car, Telscher noted, "Not a sissy people on the whole," but for a while he was as subdued as Peekskill's shabby river-edge streets rolling by. "There's a whole tradition of infamous Russian criminals. Stenka Razin, Pugachev—not that I'm comparing, but last night I was reading a little about it in those old books of my brother's." Sid smoothed back his hair and smoothed it some more: a tic. "And there was Bykov. Bykov! If he wanted someone executed, he'd bend—imagine this!—he'd *bend* two trees, tie a hand of the victim to each tree and then release the trees, dismembering the person."

Running for auditor, at peak respectability—yet Sidney remained the boy excited to know a bully, a *shtarker*. Shapes said, "This was in one of Morty's books? Which one? The OGPU manual, I wouldn't be surprised."

"And another: Two holes are cut . . . you know me: I read *everything*, whatever it is, no matter how unpleasant. Holes are cut in a frozen river about ten paces apart. Did I say this had a name? The Fisherman's Punishment. They'd tie a rope around the victim's waist. They'd stuff him down one hole and drag him out the other. Repeatedly, over and over."

"*Charles has a stereo store*." Carefully put by Sidney. Has, not *owns*. Oh, it was time, it was way past time. The money (and much much more than needed) was finally there now to snip the strings. If not Sidney, then surely Doris was wondering what Shapes was waiting for, why he wasn't discharging the debt.

"Did *you* ever want a tattoo?" Sidney was asking.

Yet Shapes suspected (more than suspected) that Sidney no more wished to be relieved of him than vice versa. Failure when shared is genial; one fool needs another; the world loves a pair—and the pair usually knows it. The Fisherman's Punishment. The Tappan Zee went by, then the Thruway; they'd come to Goshen—to the front security gates of Crescent Hill—and once more Shapes had let the subject lie sleeping. "And mark up this beautiful body?" As pointlessly, Shapes added: "Not a word from him about the shirt."

"If it'll even fit him." Sid was staring thoughtfully at his hands on the steering wheel. "Look, *I* think we did a mitzvah—but in case she ever asks: Dorie shouldn't know where we went today. What's the point of worrying her. Okay? Please. I told her it was something political."

Four hours later it was Sidney again, this time on the phone. "A bad time? I wake you from a nap?"

"I was watching television." (Shapes had been at the piano, actually.) "What's up?—but talk loudly." Since noon—at the synagogue, the halfway house, and now at home—Shapes's ears had been racketing, a ringing that wasn't going away. Playing the Bechstein a little might help, he felt, which he'd been doing when Sid phoned—the *Tempest*, a piece he set great store by. Telscher's piano business, small and independent, used to be not only south of the 57th Street piano district but also on Eighth Avenue—so when concert promoters came giving away complimentary tickets, the showroom was lucky to get what others passed up. Yet one afternoon a stooped red-haired rep named Iglauer walked in with the offer of a single unusually good seat—that same night, Carnegie Hall, Claudio Arrau—and a few hours later, in the midst of a sellout, Shapes was barely breathing as the profoundly tidy Chilean launched the ending waltz of the *Tempest* with the slightest of shoves, sending the sonata down its course on a glassy stream enveloped by a dark night.

Shapes along for the ride in the boat with Beethoven and Arrau, three men in a tub: Beethoven, Arrau, and Charlie Shapes, by some mysterious privilege the crewman, humiliated and exalted.

Ever since that evening, even to open the big Schnabel edition of the complete sonatas and turn to the Opus 31s was for Shapes to experience excitement and heart-sag at the same time. Tastable bits of today's late lunch (an onion-and-green-pepper omelet) still were crannied behind an upper tooth . . . and *I'm* going to dare to play the *Tempest* sonata? Miserably he'd touched the keys. On the other hand, six days of dogged work had made the universe—and if he just remembered to keep the music *ahead* of him, driven out of reach of his inept profaning, then little by little—shakily, unclearly—there it would reliably start to be, at least the outline of the dark rushing stream, ten bars that no one with ears would mistake for Arrau, yet which tumbled through Charles Shapes with a cleansing action, flubs and all.

Sid said, "I need to discuss something with you. It's about calling the Jewish chaplain at Pinebreeze prison, something to do with this man this morning, Roitmann."

"Why do you want to call him?"

"No, he called me."

"On Shabbos? It's still light out."

"He wants me to call him back. Are you sure I'm not interrupting anything? He knew we'd been to the halfway house. I think what he had to say is that what the Russian told us about his legal problems, the fight he had on the Van Wyck—that's only partial, it isn't the whole story. He actually *killed* someone, but somehow never went to prison. I didn't fully get it. Apparently some sort of deal was struck."

"What do you mean you think he said? Killed which someone? Who'd he kill?"

"We were just leaving the house for Rye, to go to the kids, when this Rabbi Gelman called. We were going down to watch the boys;

Lynnie had an appointment and Michael is out of town. So we had to be there on time."

"You're there, in Rye, now?" Today Shapes didn't trust his ears to pick out a distant-sounding connection from a close one.

"We didn't go, Lynnie cancelled. Here, I took down his number. Have a pencil?"

"Why do I need a pencil?"

"It's four eight five . . . you know me and these things; my knack is arithmetical, for numbers, business. *You* have the imagination for dealing with people, picking up the subtleties. You're better at something like this."

"Where's the subtlety in killing someone?"

"You know what I'm saying. The *pressures* on people."

"Four eight five . . ." said Shapes.

"Six six one two. Look, if it really bothers you—"

Shapes dialed the number from memory after Telscher got off. "I'm trying to reach the chaplain for the Jewish prisoners at Pinebreeze."

A young man's patchy-sounding voice came back with, "This is Rabbi Gelman."

"My name is Shapes. My friend is Sidney Telscher—you've spoken to him."

"Hold on a second, could you." After a moment: "I was in a bad position. All right now. Your friend told me he was going to call me right back—*three hours ago*."

"Yes, well I'm doing the calling." Shapes was all business.

"What's the difference. Your friend didn't seem that eager to give me much of his time anyway, said he had 'a household emergency.' I couldn't even start to explain this to him in two minutes, give anything more than the barest outlie*eeeeeeiiiiiinnnnnnnggggggggggeeeeeee-echwahhhhhhh*—"

Shapes wrung out his left ear violently, dislodging a clingy bud of blood-colored wax he disposed of in a piece of Kleenex from his back pants pocket. He gave an emphatic swallow, trying to direct all the free air in his head against his tympanic membranes, to still them. But it only helped a little; noise still was slicking about in there. "I'm sorry, Rabbi, please say that again."

"Counting, I was saying, the three strikes against them. Not that it's my function in the first place."

Shapes agreed "Of course"—to what, he hadn't the faintest.

"The psychologists—oh, this isn't the time to go into my feelings about psychologists. They're saying they can't declare a behavior pattern, that they don't have enough experience with Russian Jewish immigrants of this particular generation, etcetera. *I* on the other hand, who know the man—I know there *is* a pattern. The pattern is that he lies to *everybody*, not only you and your friend Mister Tischbein. That same standard story to everyone: the fight with another cabdriver, the assault and battery, legal problems—making it sound like he's out on strict parole."

The rabbi paused. Or at least Shapes thought he paused; paying less than full attention, waiting for another attack of barbarous ringing in his head, Shapes coughed twice to test if he could still hear himself do it.

"Although," the rabbi resumed, "we'll never know how the legal system would have actually looked at what Roitmann did if it hadn't been pressured by outside forces."

"Start right there," Shapes said. "Tell me what he did."

"Good, Mister *Shaa*-piss, I'm glad you want to know. Most of the others don't. Of course this is very sketchy. A year and a half before the incident with the other cabdriver, Roitmann walks in one night and finds his wife in bed with someone else—the same old stupid stupid, trite trite story. So what does he do? What any civilized person would do, right?—he stabs her. That isn't exactly accurate: actually he *saws* at her with a slicer—one of those serrated things you carve roasts with. But it's blunt-ended and what she mostly sustains are cuts. But she files charges anyway—and why not—and he's arrested, and it further comes out that this wasn't the first time for these shenanigans, that she had a lover in Russia too and Vitaly found out then also and beat her up at that time too. She was a *doctor*—did I mention that?—in a polyclinic over there, and over here I think worked in a small hospital in Queens. Three months after this incident she dies of a heart attack at thirty-eight."

All these females with heart attacks. "He mentioned something about Children's Services," Shapes said. "What is that about?"

"The daughter's in foster care," Gelman said in a hurry. "A Russian family, but I stopped keeping track. By now she may be with a second family, also Russians."

"How old is this child? Is that what you meant by pressure from outside forces? And if you don't mind, too, could you please speak just a little louder?"

"The NYANA bunch, the New Americans organization for the Russians, the refugee agencies—he's got them completely over a barrel, jumping when he calls. The first time he was arrested—you there?"

"I'm listening."

"They were called. Immediately everything was magically settled, charges dropped—and how they convinced the wife I can't imagine. But if you look at it through their eyes, these bureaucrats at the agencies had no choice. The stakes are too high for them. These Russians arrive and get a lot of good publicity: saving failing neighborhoods, enrolling in the city colleges, willing to work in the municipal hospitals as doctors or lab techs if they don't have licenses yet. For it to look like these people are also cutting each other up, just like the people they're saving marginal neighborhoods from—that's to be avoided. Too much funding is on the line, good PR at all costs is their motto. They get the charges dropped. Of course," Gelman sighed, "it's also no secret that these big Jews, these organization *machers*, love to throw weight around on general principles, for any reason whatsoever."

"Yes, that's the rap: we're generally pushy," said Shapes with sarcasm.

Gelman's voice, stubbed into a new vitality, tightened and rose: "And the *wife*, Mr. *Shaa*-piss—*she* also wasn't Jewish? Also not an immigrant under stress, plus being a *doctor*—a person who saved lives and helped people more than a Siberian radio engineer ever will? No consideration for her?"

"I'll grant you—"

"You'll grant me," the young man echoed witheringly.

"Rabbi, please come to some point—if there is one. You're obviously agitated about this, but I don't exactly see why. What's Roitmann to you and what is it you're seeking from me and my friend? You're using a lot of energy to insult someone you don't know, who visited the man exactly one single time and who isn't his guardian."

"Oh, you'll find out whose guardian you're not. You seriously believe he writes to all these synagogue men's clubs so he can discuss Yiddishkeit with them? He wants a new work sponsor. The one I arranged for him here in Peekskill isn't good enough."

"Your own legal connection to him—are you the parole person?"

"Parole? He's not even on probation! But the halfway house gets him sympathy. The deal the bureaucrats worked out after the second arrest was that he'd be on a work-release program that wouldn't even involve the halfway house. *I* am his sponsor, he's been living at *my* house and only went to the halfway program for daytime counseling twice a week—which ended almost a year ago. But now he's angry with me, we had a fight—and he wheedles the agency into letting him stay at the halfway house until he gets a new situation. Everything's a matter of manipulation with this one. Parole? I doubt if he's even on their computers anymore. He's a closed file, they couldn't give a damn. They fobbed him off on me."

"And why was that? Why you?"

"Once the professional Jews stepped in, the parole people told me flat out they saw it as a nuisance case that shouldn't go through the courts. And since I'm the Jewish chaplain at Pinebreeze prison and I was doing my thesis on Russian-Jewish emigration and I was upstate, out of the city—mostly that, I was out of the city; that was the main thing the *machers* wanted: a change of environment—so they dumped him on me. Maybe I should be happy that someone else will be stuck with him and his tantrums.

"I hope you realize what the main stipulation is as far as he's concerned. He's looking for a sponsor who'll *swear* not to send him back to the city. Though I *have* promised him that we'll go to Philadelphia—but no. His new delusional fantasy—the story changes all the time—is that the agency will make him *marry* the sister of the woman who was the first foster mother. Yet it's the child he's in terror of. The lengths he goes to. He writes letters to her that he first sends to other Russians around the country, so they'll forward them to her with distant postmarks—making it look like he's going around looking for a good job. But I, who *can* arrange a good job for him in Philadelphia—not Queens, not even the same state—I'm garbage; me he won't speak to lately. And instead of real *options*, he goes on the lookout for dupes like yourself."

"How old are you, Rabbi? Old enough I bet to know better than to insult people you don't know."

"Goes to the phone book and runs down the list of temples, trying them all. The smart ones don't even respond to the letter, but there'll always be one."

"For someone who's supposed to be a spiritual shepherd," Shapes said, "yours strikes me as a very uncharitable attitude. If I have a problem and I come to you and I want help and advice—aren't you then being *used?* Explain to me how a rabbi can see something wrong with being used if someone else needs to use you?"

"Oh Mr. *Shaa*-pizz. So saintly! I'm stung."

Less noise seemed to be in Shapes's head: a moment of surcease. "Sonny, listen—"

"Why should I listen—*you* listen! Can *I* finish speaking, if you don't mind? This desire you have to equate *my* pastoral responsibilities with your egotistical pride in doing a quote unquote good deed—this picture I'm sure you have of yourself as the big good Samaritan—my training versus your compliance in the schemings of a provenly dangerous man . . . Well, heh heh . . ."

"Now he's dangerous? Before you said he wasn't worth the court system's time."

"Heh heh. Mr. Sha-*piss*, I'm hanging up on you now and going back to sleep. None of this I see has had the sli—"

"Rabbis at seven-thirty on a Saturday night don't sleep—*or* make calls during the day."

"Whether it's because you're not *smart* enough to understand . . . but I'm going to hang up on you anyway—you *and* your recklessness."

Heart pounding morbidly, Shapes shouted, "Fuck you!" and fairly threw the receiver against its cradle before the callow little *skutz* on the other end could do it first.

4

"This being a Sunday, we don't usually open till noon, which unfortunately is why there was the mixup in communications with our engineering department." The man who spoke at the floor-stand microphone in the center of the rotunda—tall, white, young, balding, dressed in an expensive blue suit—swatted at his face. Then he removed his suit jacket, revealing red suspenders.

But few in the otherwise largely black crowd seemed to be nearly as bothered by the warm moist interior air as he was. A few of the women wore stoles. Bennett, however, was happy to follow the speaker's lead and slip his own jacket off. As far as he was concerned, the heat was truly bad. The overhead light fixtures had been shut down in favor of whatever made it through the skylights. Coming into the museum by a side entrance specially opened for the event, he and Iris had found bluntly markered blue arrows pointing the way through the dim passages of the building to the auditorium—but there they saw only darkness through the thin windows of the leather doors. Iris then had noticed a sign. "The air-conditioning's broken. They moved to the rotunda."

"Making this short, therefore, for obvious reasons: let me just say that the museum is very pleased to have you here this morning, each and every one of you. To be honoring those of you whose works are in the splendid exhibition over at Fairleigh Dickinson, a little of which—too little—we're happy to have been able to borrow and to display here this morning . . ." Milky roof light leaked down over a dozen or so paintings and pieces of small sculpture arranged on two diamond-shaped display partitions. "Again unfortunately, due to scheduling problems—"

Arriving in the neighborhood this morning, Bennett had been forced to circle and circle in search of a parking space near the museum, in the end finding something not close, across from a housing project blocks away. Without a choice, he backed in—and was just straightening the wheels when a car next to him honked its horn.

"You came!" Iris sat alone inside her Nova: it had been planned as an outing for the kids, but no child was with her, either. "Need a lift?"

Bennett leaned to speak through the Rabbit's other window. "Where will you park? There's nothing."

"Maybe not for you. Leave yours there and get in with me."

She wasn't wearing a seat belt, and her only comment to Bennett as he dug blindly between seat and door for the one on the passenger side was, "I'm not sure I'd do that." She drove directly to the museum, where she didn't hesitate to take a parking space in a side lot marked STAFF ONLY.

It was when he left the car that Bennett discovered the seat belt—wide band of grime running across his suit front from shoulder to opposite hip. "I don't know the last time someone used that belt," Iris said—not smiling but also not mortified enough as his spat-on handkerchief only smeared it. "You look like one of those road signs, those *Prohibited* signs."

Now with the jacket finally off him, Bennett felt more at ease. The floor microphone had been ceded to a pronouncedly lame black man in a denim jumpsuit and lizard loafers, one elbow tucked close to his ribs as he walked, the other poking out, paddling air. Two teased-out white sideburns—poodle tails, balls of smoke—arose from his ears. He tapped preliminarily at the microphone in front of his face. "I have just want to say . . . This work? I'm happy to be here . . ."

Deep into last night, after hours of domestic scene and upset, Bennett had wanted a glass of ice water. In her nightie, the one with the panda clutching the stalk of bamboo, Betsa shuffled downstairs to the kitchen to join him. "I am too going, Daddy," she told him, composed. "It's all settled. I am." For half a second Bennett believed her—a homely hallucination. He stroked her hair. "Well, you're wrong! I am!" she flared back. "I don't need to go to a dumb rehearsal—I knew all those steps *last* week! I'm going with you! I am!" and ran upstairs in tears. Yet that cool *It's all settled* for a moment made it seem credible, that she'd actually been a cool, reasoned negotiator with her distraught mother.

"—And like my little birds," the man at the microphone was saying. "You all know about them, my airplanes—they could be an airline some one of these days, taking souls to Heaven if called upon to do that job for the Lord."

"There's Polk." Iris didn't point, but scanning only a quarter-turn around the rotunda nevertheless gave Bennett the person she must have meant: a smallish man, younger looking than Iris but obviously a relation. Polk, the brother, seemed to be standing guard behind a seated elderly black couple. "He doesn't see me yet," Iris said. "And those are the Menenys."

"You notice no beard anymore? A dear lady friend of mine, you see, make me a present of this razor, all electric and all . . . I'm shaving with it one evening and the Lord say Jacob, Jacob, I am right here, in this hum of the razor—and right away I say back, I do know that, Lord, all machines got the Spirit in them, just resting and waiting is what they do until somebody wants to use them right and correctly."

Iris rose suddenly—"Stay here"—and sidled out of the row of chairs.

"The Lord, He going to tell you what to do and what to know and what to make—*even a lady in a red dress*." The sideburned man hooked a thumb over his shoulder at the display partition behind him. "He may *like* what she *looks* like!" (A woman's disapproving mutter of "*Evil* old man" carried from one of the rows not far behind Bennett.) "But He have got to tip me—that's all there is to that. I personally have traveled to every continent of this United States, and am an honorary colonel in the United States Air Forces, on account of my planes, and the Automoveel Club of Louisville, they did themselves a story on my boats and mostly on my planes, in their magazine which is named *Let's Go*."

During her night-long tantrum Amy repeatedly wanted to know if this revenge was original to Bennett, or was it something thought up by her father: "A girlfriend *courtesy* of him?" Then she'd be off on another staggered course, so private and broken Bennett hardly could follow (and which, when he could follow, he was barely able to stand). That she'd given up Merrit (though in fact it was Merrit who gave *her* up—leaving the country altogether three weeks ago to become the concertmaster of the City of Birmingham Symphony Orchestra, Birmingham, England) and therefore didn't "deserve" Bennett's taking advantage of her "moral strength" by doing to her what she'd done to him. For the umpteenth time: "Why otherwise wasn't *I* invited?" As Bennett's *You were*'s grew weaker, with less push to them through the night ("You, me, *and* both of the girls"), he understood what a mistake he'd made not giving Amy the three woven bags Iris had sent on as presents the week before, stashing them instead in the tire well of his Rabbit.

"Well, they're not going! They have rehearsal. And I'm not invited—don't lie! And you're not going either!"

Three and four and five times Bennett turned away, rolling over, saying "I am," and looking for sleep—if by then it was sleep that he wanted. He didn't know. Not true. He did know what he wanted. He wanted to go alone to the folk-art reception with Iris, who somehow managed to stand at or near all the doors of his current misery, whether blocking the way in or out he couldn't yet tell. He wanted to start to know how to tell. Charlie was always saying "Use your imagination"—which Bennett took as one more accusation: that men are finally expected to do exactly what they want, and that therefore Bennett must not be much of a man if he didn't even know what he might want if he ever *did* want something. He felt he ought to sleep as much as possible in case tomorrow he maybe got the chance to fuck horrid Iris and find out.

"I'm going to kill my father! A pimp!"

"Please be quiet."

"I *care*? I'm going to call him and tell him—he should know I know everything he's trying to do!" But it was easy to wrestle the phone away, and Amy's knee once going up into his belly hurt no worse than her tireless invokings of *my father*.

The poodle-headed man hurried as the museum official approached the microphone from the left. "And I talked like I am talking to you—"

Bennett saw Iris return to the rotunda through a door nearest her brother, who was startled into a jump at first notice of her.

"—*till I finished saying what I did have to say*—at the Federal Mall in Washington DeeCee in front of the Smithsonian Incorporation when they had their festival of native American artists, because you know I am also part Cherokee—"

The museum man said, "Thank you very much, Mr. Burns. . . ."

Iris was leaning down over the shoulders of the elderly seated black couple, who a second later got up to leave, the old woman pulling the old man up out of his chair. They both ultimately settled some distance away, near an obese woman in white robes who was sitting on more than one chair.

"JACOB BURNS, I TIP YOU!—the Lord says to me." (The museum man made a half-hearted grab for the microphone.) "AND IF ANYONE WANTS TO SEE MY PLANES, YOU JUST COME DOWN AND I'LL SHOW YOU THEM—"

Iris and her brother were talking with angular motions—turnings-away, doggings, more turnings-away. Iris soon after disappeared behind one of the display partitions.

"—CAUSE ABOUT ONCE A MONTH, AFTER I FILE MY FLIGHT PLANS WITH THE UNITED STATES AIR FORCE, I DO GO UP ON RIDES WITH MY FRIENDS."

The museum man wasn't going to be denied any longer; not wanting to seem to lunge, he was lunging nevertheless, and one of his hands had captured the microphone stalk.

"—ONE OR TWO OF MY LITTLE FRIENDS SHALITA OR SOMETIMES DENISE AND YOU CAN COME TOO MAYBE SOMETI—" With a peeved push—"Here!"—Poodlehead shoved the microphone into the museum man's face.

Not yet even noon and the indefinable adventure seemed to be over and done with. Bennett had almost stopped trying to follow what Iris was saying.

"Polk's mainstay always was the Chief. And Polk was the Chief's only dealer. But the Begleiters—the two dumpy little white people? she was wearing a green dress?—they're off the idea of their own museum: they've decided to open a gallery instead. So poor Polk. But it's his refusing to think about what he'll do now that worries me. We're making him a wonderful offer to be an art therapist at our school, the one Monte and I are starting, for sens-imp kids—but so far no, he's being stubborn."

Again no seat belt on her, nor this time on Bennett, though they were now in his own Rabbit (Iris's Nova had been left for her brother to use) and he was doing the driving, leaving the city, heading north.

Iris's hair flew in the breeze of her open window. Fairly often Bennett could see down her white summer dress. "You'll meet him when he's in a better mood, less deeply wigged-out than he is today. I just hope we avoid . . . —he's been hospitalized, you know, Sheppard-Pratt a few times, which is why I own half the house he lives in and why I have power of attorney along with our mother. The things he says to me! *'Aha—you want to* dance *on my grave too?'* Polk is threatened by the fact that I'm friends with Lurtha Meneny, the Chief's wife, that she's going to introduce me one of these times to Sister Ranelle. If Monte ever does the film we're thinking of making about the Chief, we're going to try to put Sister Ranelle into it also and shoot one of her healing sessions if she'll let us. *That's*, incidentally, who Charles should be going to for the ringing in his ears, not to some otolaringoolangologist. I tell him about vitamins and he smiles at me. I tell him to stop listening to music—obviously his head is giving him signals it's had too much and it's *impacted*—and he smiles at me. But instead he'll go to some quack and get dangerous drugs."

All the names: *Polk*, *The Chief*, *Lurtha*, *Sister Ranelle*. Ordinarily Bennett didn't care for people who like Iris lived so close in to their lives. It didn't occur to them that strangers need to take the tour slowly, in an elementary fashion. (Though what about people like himself who lived too far out?) The skirt of Iris's white dress puffed as she crossed her legs. Bennett said, "I'm taking you where? It'd be better about now if I knew."

The skirt got tucked beneath her, outlining her thighs, and she who never laughed laughed: "Oh!" To pick up her son, Tim—

hadn't she said? Or to at least try to, since she didn't have custody. Her ex-husband, Rick, hadn't allowed Timmy to come down with her. "Rick's a cripple—you'll see the wheelchair—so any little power he can wield . . ." Years ago there'd been a car accident. "With me driving. When I was pregnant. But I wasn't hurt. Where incidentally is *your* crew?" Bennett began, "The girls had a dance rehearsal for a pageant they're in," but Iris went on explaining that according to her ex-husband, her son was supposed to be suffering from a stomach virus picked up during the week at school. "I believe that, right?"

She rolled up her window halfway. "Apropos Charles, before I forget. A lot's on his mind and he's worried about his ears, so I'm not going to bother him about this. I thought you and me could just take care of it and leave it our secret. It's a transmitter. And another reason it's better ordered off the books is because the Barn doesn't regularly deal in it. I already checked it out and I can get it through one particular wholesaler. We'll just make it a cash transaction."

It took Bennett a moment to realize she was asking him for a *favor*, but by then she was already shooting off in another direction:

"Polk'll see once we're under way that there's nothing around even *similar* to a genuine healing school. He'll be great with these kids—he *loves* kids, he's perfect with Timmy—and the space is ideal, all that room. Much better for him than being a folk-art dealer. He doesn't have the constitution for the pressures and dealings. When his lover, Larry, staked him, that was one thing. But Larry's moved on." She sat forward to read the highway sign the Rabbit was sliding beneath. "Did that say Exit Six? We want Seven."

Off the highway Bennett was directed to smaller roads and finally to a semi-paved climbing one leading out onto a ridge, the site of three unlandscaped ranchhouses. At the third of the three, Bennett pulled the Rabbit as far right in the lane as possible, almost into a drainage ditch.

"That's Timothy there." A child in shorts and polo shirt was busily slamming a hammer against a large wooden plank on the upper reaches of a long blacktopped driveway. "And that's—" But the people Iris referred to—a woman with long yellow hair wearing a nightgownish white caftan and a man in a motorized wheelchair—quickly disappeared up a concrete ramp leading to the house. Iris opened her door and got out. Tired and nonplussed into near silence since arriving at the museum, Bennett turned off the engine and at least knew to sit still right where he was.

Iris in her sandals didn't make much noise on the asphalt as she crept up right behind the hammering boy. She bent down to kiss his head. He didn't turn. Only when she pulled at his hair did he pay initial attention—which was when Iris's hands and arms suddenly flew into motion. And the boy's too (Bennett hadn't noticed the wires streaming down from both ears to a unit attached to the belt of the boy's shorts). After their short conversation in sign-language, the boy turned his back on Iris to resume work on the plank, and she continued directly into the house through the green front door without even a glance back for Bennett.

Something as serious as a deaf son—yet never a word about it from Charlie. Possible that Bennett now knew something about Iris that Charlie didn't? The green front door opened again and this time the caftaned girl emerged. She was holding a red plastic tray and, barefoot, stayed on the driveway, avoiding the dirt front yard. When Iris's son set himself down into a glowering crouch, she passed by imperturbably, heading in the direction of the Rabbit.

Sunlight outlined the body beneath the gown; it seemed to Bennett that her nipples more than her mouth were what said hello. She looked barely twenty. "Rick thought you might like an iced coffee while you're waiting for her. We also have teas. But she shouldn't be long."

Bennett wished he'd been quick enough to open his door and scramble out before it came to this. The tray—a tall filled glass, a crystal sugar jar and crystal milk pitcher, a long-handled spoon—

was being passed through the open window into his hands. "Just leave it all somewhere down on the ground when you're done," the girl said before walking back around the rear of the car.

Now what to do with the tray? But happily Iris was back, opening the passenger-side door, although not getting in. "They've decided to make me sweat, make me *work* for my legal visitation rights." Looking at the crystal bowls: "The perfect hosts—what phonies. So you go on home, Ben. I'll get a ride somehow—maybe Monte, maybe even Polk." She looked at the tray again. "Actually, wait two seconds, all right?"

She walked up the driveway with the crystal milk pitcher in hand. When she came right behind the impervious boy, she raised and tilted it, pouring out a fast stream of milk onto Timmy's orangey-red head.

Tim jerked upward, standing with the board. His hand touched his hair, he inspected his palm—and then, an inch closer and the quick short swipe he took with the board would have knocked off Iris's head. Iris bared her teeth and made claws of her hands. Timmy spat but didn't take another swing; when Iris put down the emptied pitcher, he immediately kicked at it twice, making sure it broke. After a rapid-fire set of signs, Iris stuck her tongue out at the boy, who in a voice resembling a water pipe with pressure problems honked back what sounded like "No!" Iris's hands were palm to palm in plea, but the boy was already moving away, hitting at his hair, gathering up tools and wood and vanishing with it all around the side of the house.

"Too bad about that pitcher," Iris said when she came back to Bennett in the Rabbit. "Give me that tray, I'll take care of it. And thank you again." Nothing more, no explanation; nor could Bennett think of something appropriate to say (I'm sorry your son is deaf?). She reached inside the car to remove her woven bag. "Oh wait, what am I doing. I'm forgetting this," rummaging inside. "For you from me. And of course from the Chief. It's one of his."

It was some kind of object: a double-S-shaped piece of tin, painted red, with rawly sharp edges, resembling a partially opened Swiss Army knife in bad condition. Two punched-out holes at one end contained a pair of varnished peas. It took Bennett a moment to realize that it was meant to be a snake.

"An original Meneny. And," Iris added, "it's potent—so you be careful."

5

"Henry Hing, Vitaly Roitmann. Vitaly, Henry."

The Russian then was following Henry through the D-Lux (no one else there at that hour, two-thirty in the afternoon), holding his arms tightly to his sides and Shapes bringing up the rear.

Though Vitaly tugged at the top of it, Shapes wouldn't give over the single menu once they were seated. "All the Chinese restaurants they have in Russia, right?"

Vitaly said, "I eat plenty in Peekskill."

"You eat plastic in Peekskill. Trust me a little, I'll do us up right." And seeing the Russian wipe his neck, Shapes further promised it would be cooler in a moment, even cold—"The air-conditioning's kicking in now"—though the truth was that Shapes couldn't hear much more than his own ears, the rumble tapering and fattening inside his head on no reliable schedule. Last night had been very bad:

if he'd slept an hour it was a lot. Twice this last week he'd locked himself out of the Volvo; after the second time, he'd gone ahead and had the whole ring of keys duplicated, a second set he wore attached to his belt and nestled inside his back pocket.

Henry advanced to take the orders. "You'll like it," said Shapes, but the Russian only looked around the empty room, turning his plate occasionally like a steering wheel. After Henry departed, Shapes sighed with false comfort. "So what's with you? With your situation."

The Russian sat straighter in his chair and his hands became fists. "Augustfirst: the letter by then, you know? Coming to work for you—or else more Peekskill, more of the fucking cleaners. *Two* letters—you knew, right? One from you—with job—one from your friend—character reference of *you*." He slumped back. "But your friend he's not here." He seemed to mutter something under his breath.

Shapes tried to sound neutral about it: "He's not, no." The rabbi had frightened Sidney off. But in bed last night, trying to think of anything else but the incessant ear-whine, Shapes had arrived at a possible solution for everyone concerned. Telscher notwithstanding, a makeshift job at the Barn could be thrown together for Vitaly. Iris was forever fussing about stockroom disorder, old shipping cartons not yet broken down, paperwork lost in the mess. If Sid truly felt so uncomfortable about hiring the Russian, he would also feel he had no choice but to withdraw from the partnership, a face-saving way to at long last be bought out—at which point Shapes could neatly turn around and present the business to Bennett and Amy. Vitaly was an unlikely pivot, yet who isn't. The furniture-rental place Shapes called in the morning offered a special if Shapes could take delivery of a sofabed that same afternoon. Something temporary for the Russian to sleep on in the office. But before Shapes would tell Vitaly anything, there were things he first wanted cleared up for his own peace of mind.

"Smells wonderful!" Shapes enthused as Henry put down the soups. Then, after Henry's departure, Shapes held off picking up his spoon.

"We have a concern, Al, about the *location* of our store. For you, in your particular situation. Tortenville is farther from the city than Peekskill is. When you *do* start seeing your little girl again . . ."

Vitaly stopped eating his soup.

". . . how will it work? Are you going to want to be that far away? At least Peekskill has a train to take down."

The Russian began to eat again, slowly.

"I have a daughter too, did I ever mention? And grandgirls." Reaching into his back pocket, Shapes said, "Also a new wallet, so I hope I have pictures with me. What about you? Any pictures? I'd love to see them."

Murmuring, shaking his head, pushing aside the soy sauce/chili-oil trolley, Vitaly set down his porcelain spoon. From his own wallet and a small worn baggie inside he defeatedly pulled out three photos, upside-down at first to Shapes, who had to stick out a detaining finger when Vitaly tried slipping one of them back inside the baggie.

The smallest and oldest, aged nearly to sepia, was of a woman: a tapped-in, Vitaly-ish face, the same nose and broad neck, half smiling and wearing a very plain print dress. Shapes said "Mama?" but the Russian only turned the photo down like a card. The two others were color prints, one a Polaroid—and both of these Vitaly kept firm possession of, each to a hand, buckling them slightly between thumb and middle finger so that Shapes needed to reach over and steady the man's wrists, raising them a little for the best possible viewing. The daughter was faintly Arab-looking, eight or nine years old, tiny gold balls in her earlobes, with a nutmeat chin-dimple—someone clearly to be reckoned with, the sort of child who counts out change in a frazzled immigrant father's palm and with dignity hands it over to an impatient storekeeper.

But no matter how much Shapes felt he was prepared for whatever the third picture would show, he wasn't. The *much-ness* of the wife. The bouffant red pyre of hair, the black-rimmed eyeglasses, the spiked heels on legs sturdier than long, the lab coat straining over a figure of sexual exaggeration: big bust, big hips—an embodied plus sign. A stethoscope drooped against a thigh, limp and smirky. Shapes guessed by the presence of cars parked nearby (as well as by the cut of the lab coat) that it had been taken in front of an American hospital, and (by the quality of the light) sometime in the morning. So much provocativeness for the A.M.!

The photos jumped back into Vitaly's palms and were reinserted into baggie, wallet, and pocket. He looked at Shapes with defiance.

"*Nu?*" Shapes said calmly.

Vitaly mumbled something and violently cleared his throat. Using one of Henry Hing's thick red cloth napkins, he wiped his glasses but didn't put them back on. "Gelman tells you?"

"Tells me what," said Shapes.

He pressed both palms to his hedgy eyebrows. "All right. All right. Goodbye! Goodbye to Roitmann. Go!" he waved an airy, tragic hand. "Friend of yours not coming to me, not liking me, forget me, what the hell, right?—and now too you. So? So? So I am bad. To friends like you I don't tell truth. Howie Gelman tells you I am worthless? But you understand *why* a little bit now? Because I am ashamed. Ashamed! Is bitch, Ala—I knew this for all the time about her—but she makes me too crazy: I *love* her and she make me *more* crazy. What kind of woman this is for me?—my father goes, the only Jew, to gymnasium in Kishinev? *This* woman is son's wife, what? Crazy! Because I always *love* her."

The glasses went back on. "I do it—I hurt her—that's all—cannot be not done now. But everyone I say this to, okay? it's true, believe me: I would *die*, kill myself, for to have her come back, Ala. And Niniakin!"

Shapes said in the same calm tones, "In foster care, I realize, but exactly where is your daughter?"

"Was Queens, Rego Park—but I think this week is when they moved to Brooklyn." Vitaly suddenly looked genuinely worn. "New address is in my room, with other stuff."

"They're Russians, the family that looks after her?"

With a theatricality that annoyed Shapes, Vitaly swished this away. Shapes inched back his chair. Passive suffering (as a maestro, he should know) ought to have at least one stoic edge to it. Seeing Shapes's chair move, the Russian said, "You go?" (although the dumplings were arriving and Henry Hing looked puzzledly at Shapes). "Don't—and don't be afraid of me, Charlesshappes! Am big mess, but I can talk to you!"

"Okay, talk to me."

The Russian speared one of the dumplings and brought it to his plate; when it didn't drop free he shoved it whole into his cheek and shook his head: "Some wife Roitmann had. Some wife . . ."

"In what way."

"Everything. *Big* problem."

Shapes ate a dumpling too at this. Unable to pry. Marriage to a "big problem" he could well understand. "What about your little girl, Nina, though. Her situation. Anything *I* can do? Call her for you, check up on her, anything at all until you are back together?"

Vitaly stopped chewing and his eyes narrowed. "No job, huh?"

"Did I say anything?"

"Then *yes* a job? What?"

"The one you already have, in Peekskill, at the dry cleaners, that Rabbi Gelman arranged for you—what is the problem there?"

"Hot and stinks. No job for me."

"The rabbi says it's only temporary, right? He seems involved with you, be looking out for you."

"What means?"

"He's . . . *protective*."

Vitaly nodded his head amusedly. "*Na pravo*." (After buying a rattan throne for tonight at Pier One, Shapes today had also picked up a Berlitz phrase book in Dalton's, which unfortunately he'd left in the car.) "Offitsal," Vitaly translated.

"Official how?"

"Many many—*too* many problems—with this man." Hands and shoulders lifted in a tribal shrug: "But what can I do? He's agent."

"Excuse me? What'd you say?"

"HIAS. New Americans Committee—spies for them."

"They're not police organizations"—and when Al fixed him with a look of pity, Shapes insisted: "I know for a *fact* they're not."

Another shrug. "Okay, you know that. And *I* know what *I* know. They tell him what to do."

Shapes, realizing the misapprehension, smiled and looked up first at the ceiling. "Because they're known as *agencies*? Well, that doesn't always mean in English that they have *agents*, Al."

"They tell him to send Nina my letters from different places where fag friends of his are living. They tell him to tell me he loves me. *Loves me.* Wants to suck my cock, that's what he loves!"

"Wai . . . wait . . ."

"Yes, *Howie Gelman.*"

"Wants to—?" Henry and Mrs. Hing were approaching with dish after dish.

"Suck my cock. All he wants."

Shapes said "Ah, look how glorious this food is! Look at all this, will you! Start eating!"

"And wants me to fuck him in the—"

"Eat before it all gets cold!"

Fortunately Shapes didn't have much time to think about it later. He had to make ready for Judge Leona. As soon as everyone was gone from the Barn, he hunted in the stockroom for adhesive tape—something to keep the sheet of cardboard tight over the narrow window in the office—and while doing that had the indistinct impression of fewer, smaller stacks of cartons in the hot dark area. Either business was suddenly better, or Iris in fact had gone ahead on her own, done some cleaning up . . . or else this was an opening-out. On the slim chance it was (a mini), he lifted a pointing finger, to see if the finger would seem to elongate, distort.

It stayed put. Last week, having finally gone to a local ear man about the ringing, Shapes had made casual mention of the peeling-back experiences. But the doctor wasn't impressed: perhaps it was a balance problem, which might fit in with the primary complaint—but these things were hard to pin down exactly, sometimes even after investigation. Templeton, the doctor, who looked to be about his own age, used a suction device and a gleaming pair of pincers to go at the wax in Shapes's ears, not the warm-water syringe and kidney pans of previous cleanings. As the suction *brrr*ated by Shapes's eardrum, Templeton shouted, "Getting all this stuff out of here ought to help considerably." Yet he must have known it would do no such thing. And Shapes knew he knew—the semi-failed sniff each other out. The appointment was at Templeton's "satellite" office, not the telephone book's primary listing, an office in Kingston. Every time Shapes had tried calling there, it got him the other office instead. That turned out to be a storefront suite situated, like the Barn, in a mini-mall; the only other tenant, next door, was a sneaker outlet. Shapes wrote out a check as Templeton said, "This noise thing sometimes works like headache—in clusters. You'll have it for a time and then one day notice you don't anymore. Tinnitus is hard to pin down to one etiology. Acoustic nerve tumor. Brain tumor. Hypertension. Any problems with your pressure?" Yes, the failed identify each other, and five minutes after Shapes left, as he was sniffing the faint smell of fresh Keds trapped within the Volvo, the rough ear whine returned, no more improved than before.

After he taped the cardboard over the window and set up the lighting umbrella approximately in place, Shapes was tired and sat down at the desk. The accusation about the rabbi aside, just the picking up of the Russian in Peekskill, the taking him to lunch at the D-Lux, and the driving back to Peekskill one more time had been a lot for Shapes after a night of no sleep.

All things being equal, how *would* Vitaly fit in here? Perhaps he'd be useful even. For, with Bennett running the show, Iris would probably go. Maybe willingly: from her occasional remarks about it, the day-care center or whatever it was that she was involved in seemed ready to open. Still, Shapes would not want to be the one ushering her out. He was grateful to Iris. Despite the personal phone calls she made, the mysterious time she took off, and the pilfering, she'd been valuable, especially in the beginning, rooting out what was left of the rent-to-own policy, moving the focus over to deep discounting on mid-to-low-range items. The new trucker she'd arranged for seemed to be working out well, too, delivering when he promised—though she still claimed to be unhappy about haphazard invoicing.

Yet there was no possible way she could remain. Iris gave Bennett hives; around her he became stiff and humorless. The three of them had been in the office the other day after closing. Iris had remarked, "You need a haircut, Charles. You're getting backcurls," and Shapes had asked, "Are they at least distinguished-looking?" "*Greasy*-looking." "How can that be? My hair is if anything too dry—I flake." "Flaking comes from oiliness too. You need more folic acid. Probably also some D and E."

Normally whenever Shapes and Iris bantered, Bennett would do something like grab a cloth and a can of Endust and make himself scarce. But this time he had stayed put, as if frozen.

"You don't believe me," Iris said, "—but you will when I show you something," pulling at Shapes's hand. "Come over here and take a look."

"Looking."

"But not seeing." Clumsily she hauled Shapes's chair out of the desk well, the casters going left when she wanted them going right. "What do you see there?"

"This is a wild surmise . . . —but a chair."

"Right *here?*"

"The back of the chair, the *top* of the back of the chair?—am I getting at all warm?"

"The *color.*"

"According to the catalogue," Shapes recalled, " 'Dark Chocolate.' "

"And here?"

"Everywhere. Brown all over."

"Come on, Charles, it's not—over here it's *black!*"

"Where my head rests," Shapes agreed. "I have dark thoughts." (But not so much as a grin from Bennett.)

"It's black, Charlesie—from *oil*. The oil in your hair. Doesn't that tell you anything? Folic acid. D and E—that's your prescription. Or else you better get one of those things they have on airplane seats—"

It was possible of course that he hadn't heard right. But she repeated it: "An antimassacre."

"What do you suppose she means?" Shapes turned to Bennett. "The U.N. peacekeeping forces? The National Rifle Association?"

"That cloth they drape over a headrest. Oh, all right, come on, you two *never* mispronounce a word."

"When the subject is pogroms we try to avoid it, right Bennett?"

Iris slung a hip to wait Shapes out: "Very funny, very funny"— and yet even *then* poor bollixed Bennett didn't enter in: stood there, a statue without reaction, not even a smile. No, there wasn't a way Iris could stay.

Shapes got up, for there were still last things to prepare, to do before Leona got here. The floor vase of reeds (also from Pier One) needed to be placed beside the rattan throne. And the reflecting umbrella rearranged. He was just going to test the floodlight when the phone began to ring (or he hoped it was the phone).

"Is this Charles?"

"No, it's Moishe Pipick—and is *this* person Amy, my only spawn and dearest daughter?"

"Mister Shapes . . ." After a short ridgy hesitation: "This is Leona Mackey."

"Onlona! I— excuse me: Leona!"

"About our appointment tonight. You remember meeting my husband, so you understand. I'm the chauffeur, and he's got a very important unexpected meeting he has to attend tonight. Our tax-protest group. Since I can't enter in, Fred speaks for us both there—though of course people know where I stand."

Shapes's ears took over for a moment, and he missed a few words of what was said next. " . . . but the taxers just keep going their merry way, don't they? We beat them down but they come back for more. Another school levy, two point five mill. Fewer and fewer children in the district, yet constant levies. They must think we're idiots. Sheep. I personally put it down to the fact that before committees like ours no one dared to say no to them. Fred and I see it as the last shred of democracy in this country. Am I right?"

Shapes said he'd always been under the impression that school levies were *good* things, but perhaps had been naive.

"Get into Monte Vogelsang's group then—he'll open your eyes for you. Monte's a dear, and so intelligent; he realizes that there's something sacred about individual ambition. That's why he calls the entrepreneurs' group a ministry. Join and you're ordained. Legally. There is a legal certificate."

"Are you? Ordained, I mean?"

"It's only for men so far. Go on up there. I mean it. He holds services every Wednesday night. Property owners and small businessmen: that's where the buck stops. Tax increases year after year after year—it's a form of blackmail, you realize. They roll right over you, the so-called 'educators.' But we showed *them* two years ago. We closed the schools—two and a half months, the parents crying bloody murder, their precious little tykes!—but we held fast and got rid of the crucial troublemakers, the teacher-union agitators. *Then* we opened up again, only after that. People don't appreciate that property levies never *ever* dissolve. Right? Did I inconvenience you very much about tonight?"

"Not much," Shapes said.

"I'm glad."

"Just a little."

"Well, if I can do it another time I'll certainly call you. But now I've got to run: a lot of things to do. That meeting, as I said."

"I appreciate your calling, letting me know."

"Another time?"

"Oh, of course."

Telscher kept a bottle of imported vodka in the office's half-refrigerator in case of palpitations when he paid his less and less frequent visits. Shapes got it out, poured a little into a paper cup, and lay down on the unopened new sofabed. Was he sorry? As much as he would have liked to renounce his habit of renunciation, life tended to have other ideas. Vitaly's photograph of the blowsy wife came to mind—and what if Judge Leona had turned out to be that variety of lollapalooza? Fatigued as he was, without sleep the night before, he couldn't have kept up. What he needed more than sex was sleep, the peace of sleep, and sipping the vodka made him drowsy, so much so that even the ear noise seemed half-restful, lulling. Though he would have been at least curious to see her makeup case: to unclench its brass teeth and dig in, first playing the role of the inspector, fisting up lipsticks and blusher, puffs and liner, round mirror; encouraging, being constantly encouraging while she rubbed a sponge over her jaw and they talked about the Telschers. *I remember my own first time out, running.* She'd also been slated to run for auditor, but then county clerk turned up instead. —Work it way up, as much up into the hairline as you can—watching her skate the sponge along the side of her large face—and don't forget down there—the base of her throat, handing her a mirror as she moved next to her brows, silver pendant earrings, a silver chain looped twice around her neck. The reeds brush at her arms, so he moves them a little. *Is this all right?* —Perfect, maybe just a little too much by the side of your nose . . . —handing over a handkerchief. *Is that a bathroom over there or a closet?*—and taking her bag in, she emerges later barefoot in a red leotard, tights of the same shade, another string of pearls added, one more silver chain (on the left ankle—very Ala-Roitmannish), and sits as directed on the rattan planter's chair, breasts with a fetching sag, aureoles under the spandex high and wide as a stack of poker chips. *Will I know when you actually begin taking?* Hunching a little in modesty, gripping the woven lip of the seat edge, a very slight tire around her middle, especially when bending at the waist, thighs that give the tights no rest. —Can you do something with your hands for me?— *What?* —Anything you like.— *This?* —Touch your face. Make a sort of sling for your chin with the backs of them—and he flicks on the floods. —Turn your butt just a little, a quarter turn to the left will be dandy— With *butt* a look of special watchfulness comes into her eyes. The left hand on the knee stays as is. He suggests sliding it: —Up your thigh, the same one, the right one, that's it, about halfway up, but don't move it back and forth like that, I'm only taking stills. Good, like that. You're starting to look like you're enjoying yourself— She is, *but it's a little hard on my back this way.* A breast thrusting forth with each therapeutic flex of her spine. *How about my knees up together but to the right—because I want to be compact enough to get into the lens there.* —Good.— *And if I twist my middle something like this? And also what about my big feet—aren't they showing too much?* Spotlamp-sweat dewing her collarbone, purple halfmoons under the arms of the leotards, and suddenly she leaves the pose, sitting straight again, gripping the armrest.

I hope you'll take this in the spirit I mean it and won't misunderstand

. . . A philosophical discussion follows: will the actual, physical film rightfully belong to her because it's *of* her, or to Shapes because it was shot *by* him? You're that ashamed of doing this? he teases, but she comes right back: *What would be the fun if I weren't?* It's agreed that she'll have the film when they're done.

And what if, say, this is the moment when she rises to go behind the chair's high back? She returns with nothing on, forcing Shapes to bend to the camera's viewfinder to reduce her overwhelmingness while she quickly gets back onto the chair: —Lights on!— She grabs for the reeds, a double dozen, camouflaging her lap, —One more light, ready?— and she squeals, covers her eyes and uncovers her chest, the reeds roll off, lap-beard revealed and inner thighs, and now he must work quickly, —Here's this—, a sheet of cream-colored, deckled stationery found around the house and a long pen, a manufacturer's giveaway, SATO—FIRST IN SOUND. What he'd like her to do is cross her legs, the pen to her lips in thought, thinking what she'll write, —A letter, if you want— *Oh, I like this.* She once did some community theater. *What if I put them like so?*— lifting her legs, revolving her bottom so that her calves hang like a face towel off the side of the chair, and then turning away from the camera altogether, briefly standing, then kneeling with the paper held high, turning back once more, announcing *Here's my letter so far,* but quickly scribbling something else too, sailing the paper expertly through the air until it hits the base of the tripod: *Dear Charles, couldn't you come over here, closer, when you're all done, and touch me?* He leans to give back the paper, —Not at the moment—, and there's another furious scribble: *Should I maybe touch myself in the meantime? Are you telling me to do that?* and she sighs and rests the pen and paper at her feet . . . although she's not the judge/merrywidow anymore but Ala Roitmann, more the Whore of Babylon than he likes, but too late now, he's on the way, pulling rubbing going, until someone's question— *"Charles?"*—causes his hand to fly off himself.

"Iris?"

Shapes, struggling to his feet, could see he wasn't the only startled one. As Iris moved hesitantly into the office from the stockroom, her brown-freckle/white-skin complexion contrast was at full wattage. After looking briefly back toward the stockroom, she said, "Were you sleeping?"

Shapes indicated the paper cup: "Half and half: a little drink, a little dream," then sat and immediately crossed his legs. "Half-conscious. If I could hear anything anymore, you would have scared me to death. What did you do, come in through a window?"

She stared quizzically at the umbrella, the lights, the rattan throne, the reeds upon the desk, the sofa beneath him. Shapes urged her to have a seat—"Plenty of room"—and she chose the empty planter's chair.

"I was out looking for cartons—for when we finally move into the school—and I was driving by and saw lights on in back. The window looked strange. Why is it covered over like that? Why are you here so late? When I came in, it looked to me like— . . . Were you playing with yourself, Charles?"—slipping off her sandals.

Shapes shook his head in amazement. "Your *delicacy*, Iris."

"No, it's okay, Charles—we're able to talk to each other. We're alike."

"I should hope we're alive."

"*Alike*. We'll have adults too, you know, at our school for the deaf. It won't only be for children."

Shapes hurriedly stood up, turned around, and zipped up before sitting back down. "In what ways are we alike?"

"We're celibate, for one. A lot of people nowadays are."

"There was an article in the *Times* about it. What's behind it, you suppose—fear of catching disease?"

"Well, why are *you*?"

"Why am I what? Celibate? I'm not. I can certainly sympathize, though. The body is so capricious. With my ears lately, I only know too well that it seems to want to be rid of *you*, to swallow you. You'd like to try to get even with it by ignoring it." To calm himself and sand down the edges of his surprise, Shapes took a sip of his vodka. "But that doesn't work either."

"People aren't machines, Charles. They don't 'work.'"

"*Celibate*, Iris—really? You have a son."

"Only one; you don't see me keep having them. You don't *have* to admit to me that you're celibate, Charles."

"Do you play with *your*self?"

Shapes had tried to shock her, but she was amused instead. "I think I asked first. Sure I do. Sometimes." (Nothing unnerved her. Poor Bennett for this reason found her so unnerving.)

"This conversation," Shapes sat straighter on the sofa, "is a first, I have to say, for me."

"You're doing well at it."

"Thank you."

"And it's requiring courage. But it's well known that when you lose a sense you find others. My son is very *very* brave—people notice all the time—and the reason he is is because he isn't distracted, he can focus. Why do you think I'm always bugging you about music?"

"Hello again music."

"You have to defend yourself, to *focus*—and music's no help. Will you at least admit that most people at a concert are passive, won't think for themselves?"

"They're concertgoers, not gladiators. Anyway, who says thinking is necessarily the point of going to a concert?"

"Then what is?"

"I'm not insensitive, Iris. I can understand why—with your son and all—you might have this attitude—"

One bare foot stamped formally against the floor. "You *are* insensitive, but don't change the subject. The subject isn't me or my son but the negative auras of music."

"The guards whistling Mozart in the concentration camps, you're going to tell me."

"Did they do that?"

"I'm sorry but despite all that the people who pay money to hear a chamber music concert are the kind of people you wouldn't mind asking to watch your wallet for five minutes. Good characters, on the whole."

Iris crowed: "*Wallets!* My point exactly. What makes music lovers so special? They have memories? They're flattered to sit there and anticipate what they've heard before. That isn't character. That's *hoarding.*"

Shapes shook his head in disagreement. "They're taken *out* of themselves for an hour and a half—something not so terrible. How much chance do people have to take a moment away from themselves. Say it is even a little self-congratulatory, to like something better the second time you hear it than the first—that's such a crime? At least sitting there you feel that the secret is coming *at* you rather than *from* you. It checks the ego. A rare experience. Intimate."

Almost with a straight face, Iris said, "So's masturbating."

Shapes was able to do little about his blush. "How do *you* do it?" he countered.

"Do what?"

"You know."

"This whole time, by the way, since I came in (and I've been speaking extra low), you've heard everything I've said. Because you're paying *attention.* I take a pillow and I lie down over it."

"Show me. I can't picture it."

"Oh, sure I will!"

"Celibates can't also be dirty old men?"

"What *is* all this stuff?" On her feet again, Iris was gesturing at the photo paraphernalia, the new furniture.

"I was about to shoot photos of equipment for an ad. Want to be in an ad, holding a turntable?"

"Only with clothes on."

"Two celibates like us, what would it matter?"

"No more vodka for you, Charles." She slipped on her sandals. "Or maybe you *should* have more."

"Sit down, don't go yet. Tell me about your boy. Actually, first: really, what were you doing here at this hour? How did you see light coming through the *back* window?"

"I came to steal you blind, Charlsie—to take everything."

"Every pencil? All my stationery?"

"Just empty cartons. Actually, there was something else I wanted to check on. A particular invoice," she said, "that I can't track down. But it's complicated. I'll tell you tomorrow."

"No, try me." Combining with the lack of sleep, the alcohol left him quite punchy. Shapes lay back on the sofa. "If you were to come through the back, which I'm assuming you did, the alarm would have gone off. Did it? I didn't hear it. I was on the phone." He arranged his arms over his head and closed his eyes. "Anyway, I'm glad you're here. There's something we have to at least start to talk about—"

"Charles, really I have to go. I'm sure it'll keep till tomorrow. I'll let myself back out through stock."

"—a rearrangement."

"And you go home too. Don't stay here all night and drink and diddle."

With eyes still covered and closed, Shapes laughed. "Someone else will be working here soon. And what may happen in that case—"

"And don't forget to do up your fly."

With a blind hand Shapes checked, though he remembered redoing it. "It's closed." He laughed again. "Getting back to bodies—to get back to that. They're supposed to be our servants, but they're not. Even though they acted like servants when we were young. Then, though— Iris?"

Shapes opened his eyes. She wasn't in the room. She had left.

6

Again he found himself rifling the drawers of Charlie's desk when no one else was around (Iris gone to lunch, Charlie away at the doctor for his ears, and needless to say no customers). Bennett acknowledged it was unattractive, this late habit of his, but refused to blame himself entirely—should he be the only one here who wasn't furtive? (Iris and Charlie were master mysterians both.) He never looked for anything specific; it was the simple act of going through Charlie's personal places that gave an almost physical satisfaction.

It was, besides, the ony *defensive* maneuver at his disposal, and without it his life might be pure—and purely exhausting—reaction. To come to work here meant to wait always for some new surprise, some bit of previous planning he'd been kept totally in the dark about. If not something outrightly distressing then at least bizarre, unaccountable. A sofabed, for instance, all of a sudden appearing in the cramped-to-begin-with office; or a call like yesterday's for Iris, while she was out to lunch: her brother wanting to know whether Bennett could provide him with "any, any help in locating the serpent."

"Excuse me?"

"The Meneny serpent," the brother repeated.

Bennett remembered Iris saying her brother had had a history of mental problems. "This is the Sound Barn, in Tortenville. You sure you have the right number?"

In a high, frightening voice the brother wailed: "I bet *not*! What *is* the right and perfect number?"—and hung up.

And then there was yesterday's piece of news, dropped on Bennett like a damp sheet needing ironing in a hurry: that in a week—or at the latest the week after that—someone Bennett didn't know—a Russian, *a Russian who'd been in prison*—was coming to work here at the Barn.

Difficult under the best of circumstances, questioning Charlie about his plans and projects (and hoping for any kind of answer) was inconceivable now. A nagging ringing in his ears kept him up nights, he claimed; and during the day he did seem logy, more insulated and immune than usual.

What option then, what other avenue for self-respect, did Bennett have but to snoop?

Normally very little accumulated between his searches, but today Bennett did discover two new things, both of them lying beneath a pile of recent bills. On a slip of sharply folded paper was the word *Leona* and a phone number—Bennett assumed it was the last name of the Russian who was coming. The other was more intriguing: a memo-pad sheet, Charlie's handwriting on it, "Show to Bennett." A brochure on thick, unctuous paper like vellum was attached by a paperclip.

On closer inspection, though, it too was disappointing. (Anything would be, he had to admit, that wasn't, say, a diary, or hurried love note, even a satisfied scrawl on a scrap: *Put it into Iris so quickly this afternoon that she gasped.* Or better still: *Didn't put it into Iris today.* Or, best—since Bennett was beginning to doubt Charlie ever had had anything physical to do with Iris—*Iris tells me she's perplexed why Bennett doesn't come on to her, doesn't take her to bed.*) No: looking at the brochure, Bennett recognized it as something Charlie had once mentioned having to do with Iris's ex-boss, Monte, with the Woodstocks: The Church of The Continuum, East Dorchester, New York. The cover featured a photograph of a circle of hand-holding, long-haired middle-aged men in robes, djellaba-like things.

Bennett strained his eyes to see whether there was a woman in the picture, and if it was Iris. There wasn't. Inside, the text had phrases like "the ineffability of human will," "free expression through the open, joyous marketplace," and "entrepreneurship-as-ministry." At the end it was noted that further information could be obtained from the following: The Luscious Rind Cheese Shop, WRVW Radio, Inner Health Vitamin Distribution Co-Op, and Vee's (formerly Abou Ben Adhem) Restaurant, all in East Dorchester.

Once more Bennett turned to the brochure's front. All the nincompoops in the picture were definitely male, none of them was Iris . . . though who's to say she wasn't patiently standing just out of camera range with that pain-in-the-ass expression on her face of being above and beyond, yet also central to, absolutely everything.

And in that case, would she have also been wearing one of these ridiculous robes?

For that matter, would she have been wearing *anything*?

J_U_L_Y

7

Hot, Vitaly thought, suffering.

The crapped-on stand for it so hot. Everyone else, with this weather, at least they were able to wander out into the air if they wanted to, walk around for a little coolness. But even if he trusted himself to get back inside the store, where was there to walk around here?

Hot. Air-conditioning—but not good air-conditioning. Like a room: you walk in and out but it doesn't follow. And this fucking *mattress*, like soft wet paper, especially down around the feet. Even the halfway house beds were better than this. Here his head definitely feels like it's tipping back. Only the crapped-on, the fucked-with. To top it off, his clothes are in three shopping bags so thin they all can fit between the arm of the sofabed and the office's file cabinet.

He sits up and puts his feet on the floor. Charlesshappes never said not to make phone calls; the son-in-law and the manageress didn't say he shouldn't either. In fact, no one said anything to him all day, period: what he could do, what he couldn't. His first day, what he thought was liberation, his escape from Gelman—and right away disaster.

Besides, even if he could go out for some air, what about the manageress—she said she'd be back soon, and for this reason his pants are still on. At the desk, while he still has time before she gets here, he dials the phone. Two rings (his heart stamps), three, four—but if by some chance they are going to pick up, he is just as likely to hang up as to squeal embarrassedly *"Allo? Gavareet Talik! Pajalasta saydyenyete myeye s'Nina!"* After which it would only be thirty seconds, no more, until the lousybitchcunt—once she's said nothing to him for a very long time—comes out with the lie that Nina isn't there, is out. She's always out.

He hangs up quickly before an answer. No use. Howie by now probably climbs over everything, speaks to everyone—that I left Peekskill, left *him*, for here—and is telling everyone stories and lies so that *more* of them can be against me. Gelman, like Ala, loves to scold more than loves to love. To love for this type *is* to scold, to play severely with a doll—and if the doll is a *person*, even better.

Someone on the other hand like Charlesshappes—who does not treat people like dolls but like men instead: what ends up happening to such a person? Pale, no color, bad-enough-looking when he comes to the halfway house to bring me here for the first day of work and staying, but then worse: the sweating Charlesshappes did all morning, sitting at his desk staring at the walls and finally falling down, head dropping, hitting the desk. (My opinion—a doctor's husband's—is stroke. But no one asks.)

He returns to the crummy mattress. Maybe the red-haired manageress won't return, will leave him alone. He isn't hungry for food. Where all of them are wrong—good like Charles, bad like Gelman, in between like Ala—is to want to treat instead of be treated. To decide what to do and who to do it to, looking always for new victims. I settle on the other hand for being treated. *Your* shoulders, *your* back, *your* ass will be hit—but always your identical places, no surprises, and always *you*.

This redhair, if she's coming back expecting him to do more than eat her food, she'll be sorry: a damp cheesy smell steams up from the blanket as he settles back beneath. The old heavy blanket stinks too. (Charlesshappes had said something about getting a small shower installed, but no chance of that now.) It is depressing.

One of the drivers in the garage, Frank, the one who lent everyone swami pamphlets, once gave him an exercise against being depressed, which involved *thinking* a happy dream. Twist your mind, Frank said, into a paper cone and fill it up. He tries, but instead only rehashes last night's dream: A man and woman, someone tall, dark hair, with a thin face (like Zina Aristarkhovna's, the quiet, naive one who lived in the apartment of Ala's slutty radiologist friend Lenochka; or Mrs. Hart's, from the *Hart to Hart* reruns, his favorite show), in a white fur and high dark brown boots. They are walking up a very very high bridge. It's snowing. He crowds her up against one of the girders the white fur coat opened tugging up the waist of the dress pants pulled down putting it into her . . .

No, too soon.

They walk on the pedestrian lane. She tells him she isn't cold, but she lies. They find other citizens congregated at the middle for the scenic view. He and the woman remove their coats (not only are they above the weather but they have the sensation that they are *better* than it), and the woman becomes playful, shrugging out of her white fur and flinging it toward him by a sleeve, for him to catch. But it comes at him before he's ready, flying around his head instead of landing in his hand, and he swats at it—defending himself—and finally manages to send it back to her like a ball. However she is looking over the railing, at the clouds below—and the coat falls past her over the railing, down into the tops of clouds. Her angry eyes want to know why he didn't try to snag her coat. Is he a jerk, a fuckup, to just watch it fall like that into the clouds?

A noise is coming from the other side of the wall, the storeroom. If it's the manageress, she would have keys to the front. So who is it? Gelman? Motionless as the dead: *I'm not here.* Or a robbery? (They'll say I was part of it, involved. Yet do I have a car? What could I steal?) The bed groans when he moves, singing hello Pinebreeze, hello death—but all he can do is turn his face away, the blanket over him, as the footsteps approach the office door.

"Al, are you sleeping?" The redhead is wearing a yellow shirt and holding a paper bag. "Lights were off, so I thought maybe Bennett came by after all."

He sits up partially. "Mister Wyler calls here before. Says that Charles goes to hospital, to the *other* hospital."

"Yeah, Bennett let me know too: out of cardiac care. Though I could have told them that was never the problem. What about you? You okay? A crazy, crazy day. I brought the food." She looks inside the bag: "Seven-grain bread. The filling is hummus, tomato, lettuce, plus three fat slices of really good Vermont cheese—my friend owns a cheese store." When she opens it a smell of cypress-wood releases.

"He looked very very bad," Al notes about Charlesshappes.

"What does he expect them to find in a *hospital*, though—even down at NYU—testing his ears. The timing, I agree, was definitely rotten. Some first day for you: Charles collapsing, you forced to sleep here at night—"

Anxious to clarify that this was how it was supposed to be, that she mustn't be thinking of throwing him out, he begins, "This *was* the arrangement—" but she isn't paying attention. Instead, handing over the paper bag, she gets busy inside a large tote bag she's also brought.

"Not even a proper blanket," handing him a white and red lightweight quilt, finding a spot for herself then on a corner of the desk (the open bed takes up much of the room). "For the time being, meals for you is going to have to be my department. I'm sure you're used to better food in Russia than what you'll get here—more natural. But I'll try. There isn't even anything like a decent restaurant you can walk to."

He opens the bag. If she'd only go now, he would throw away the disgusting sandwich. What is she waiting for? He has a cramp from holding himself so compactly under the covers, beginning in the muscles below both knees and spreading in spikes into throat, neck, and back-of-the-head pains. While she is snapping out the quilt, he turns further on his side—to stretch and, more important, to set the sandwich bag on the floor.

"We forgot to tell you where the thermostat is and how it works, didn't we?" She fans herself with her shirtfront. When he explains that he was told but finds the air-conditioning too noisy and would rather be without it, she says, "Still, it's too hot in here. Charles says you were a radio engineer. I used to work in radio too. The same friend who owns the cheese shop? His radio station."

"Engineer?"

"Announcer. Did you work for Radio Moscow?"

"Technical services." He launches into his well-worn story. "For military purposes—"

She is fanning herself with her blouse. "That's extremely interesting. We get told that anyone with defense or security or military backgrounds isn't allowed to ever leave. But you were free to. Plenty of what we're told I'm sure isn't true—they're so afraid here that people might realize Russia's as good a place to live as anywhere else. At least there you don't have people starving. Except for you."

He is starting to have to pee. Also it has turned terribly hot under the blanket.

"They seem if anything more open-minded over there. Work they do for instance on Kirlian photography and other parapsychology research. Here they'd never fund an institute for Kirlian photography, it would make the quote unquote real scientists angry, yet all you hear is how depressing Russia is, how conformist. In the ways that *really* count, you were probably *freer* over there."

He shrugs, "I don't know," willing to tolerate this as long as it keeps her from urging him to eat the sandwich.

"Do they use Kirlian photography there as a *diagnostic* tool too? Do you know? In deafness research? I bet they do. Aura documentation like that." And in the meantime she has somehow gotten hold of the blanket's edge and is starting to pull the whole thing off him. "Don't be shy; I can see that your pants are on."

But as he fights to get the blanket back, he accidentally slaps her elbow. She drops the blanket, smiling, to slap him back against the hair of his chest, and completely without thinking he punches at her elbow again. She laughs—"Ow, that hurt! This the way they train bears in a Russian circus?"—and seems to let go of the blanket, allowing him to rearrange it modestly over him. But then her hands shoot out and grab hold again, giving the blanket a mighty pull—"*Ooof!*"—and she falls on top of him when he won't let it go.

During the next few minutes, it seems to him that the sandwich bag must have overturned, and in the end, partly because of the terrible stink, he cannot spurt. But at least the manageress is happy—the type who likes to get pounded, the harder and faster the better; who likes to disappear flattened into it and who is curious to see what you can do, who likes to see if she's guessed right. She's very happy that he hammers away, neck at a difficult angle against the sofaback in order to move her knees so that they touch her temples; and after that, when he keeps her flat until she makes contortions and painful grips on his arms. She vulgarly holds herself down there afterwards and he apologizes for the roughness.

"You should be—it hurt. Didn't you come?"

"I—"

"Charles said you had a daughter."

And though the last thing he wants to do is say the name, he says it—"Nina"—which right away she plays with, stretching it at the same time her body stretches—"Nina, Neee-na"—enough to make him sick, Nina's name while the woman's bags are shifting, while she is still smeary.

"I have a child too, but a boy. How old is Nina?"

He tells this too—jerk and fuckup that he is—but at least he lies: "Nine."

"Nine is wonderful. Timmy and Nina could become friends like we're friends now. Timmy is also nine. It's wonderful. I don't suppose Charles ever got time to mention Timmy yet, so I'll tell you a little about him. . ."

8

"Still here," Shapes told Amy when she returned from the billing office. "No Siegel yet."

Amy sat directly down on the edge of the bed, fluttering a long piece of computer paper dangling from her hand. "This is ridiculous."

"He'll be here. He told me last night I could leave today."

"*This*." She shook the bill. "I thought I went over it carefully down there, but this I missed. Look at this."

"Later," said Shapes.

"Seven hundred and twenty-eight dollars for audiometric tests? How did I miss this? Can it possibly be right? Take a look."

"When we get home."

"No, this is absurd." Amy got to her feet. "I'm going down and try to get an explanation."

Not two minutes after she'd gone, one of the nurses came in to tell Shapes that Dr. Siegel was in-house, but finishing up a case in the O.R.; as soon as he was done he'd be up to sign Mr. Shapes out. If lunch came in the meantime, while he was still waiting, he by all means should eat it. "Paid for," Shapes acknowledged amiably. "You got it," the nurse cocked a finger.

He'd already looked out the window, read the paper, walked the halls a few times: he was running out of things to do while he waited. His only book, now packed up in the suitcase, was a life of Beethoven. Taken with him to the hospital in a spasm of self-pity. But reading the Heilingenstadt Testament, 1802—the end of deafened Beethoven's tether—". . . *My misfortune is doubly painful to me because I am bound to be misunderstood; for me there can be no relaxation with my fellow men, no refined conversations, no mutual exchange of ideas. I must live almost alone, like one who has been banished; I can mix with society only as much as true necessity demands. If I approach near to people a hot terror seizes upon me, and I fear being exposed to the danger that my condition might be noticed* . . ." And: ". . . *Perhaps I shall get better, perhaps not; I am ready.—Forced to become a philosopher already in my twenty-eighth year* . . ."—only made Shapes feel worse. Being philosophical before he *needed* to be was the chief error of Shapes's life—a passive resister, wetting matches before they flamed—and he sympathized with Beethoven's depression at the prospect. But Shapes wasn't Beethoven, had no original melodies to be deserted by, had comically less to lose, unless you counted the peelings-back—and they were dwindling on their own. Shapes's last decent one had been in Lauderdale, and even that was suspect: sleeping in Elise's bedroom the first night after her death, alone in her boundless bed until insomnia finally drove him from it, he'd turned on a lamp, gone across the room to the closet and pulled from its hanger one of Elise's housecoats and put it on. Between fabric and skin there seemed to be a *climate*, slightly different zones; if he cocked an arm, fabric didn't hug his biceps immediately. It made for a distinct sandwich: Shapes-skin, interior air like underwear, and ultimately the cloth of the housecoat—and he'd started to cry. That was that, the big peeling-back: hardly worthy of the name.

He wondered if Beethoven, deaf, had had tinnitus too. Could all that subsequent music have been a sublime noise meant to drown out some other? The night before the morning of his collapse at the Barn—the surf in his head driving him crazier by the minute—Shapes had played all night with the idea of a last dinner of pills or a session in the Volvo, holding a hose attached at the other end to the tailpipe. Yet he was too shy for suicide, the corniness and ostentation, like those Music Minus One records he used to play his piano to: your own safe solo, but backed by the Cosmic Orchestra, without any risk whatsoever of an audience. Yet if not suicide, then something. The tinnitus had taken on an alarming new quality, a screaming tone tacked to the usual roughened roar, and that night in particular the scream seemed more precise, narrowed, higher. Shapes was sure it was the cry of a blood vessel about to burst and at 2 A.M. called Templeton, but was connected to his service. The doctor was out of town.

Desperate, Shapes had clutched at a suggestion Templeton once made, something reserved, he said, for when the noise seemed especially unbearable. A tape-recorder. "Have one?" "A hundred—at the store." "You only need one. Try this: Talk into the microphone, and when you play it back, do it at full volume. Make sure you hear yourself above your ear noise. It'll remind you there's still a you under there, that you're more than your noise, difficult as that is for you to appreciate now. Siegel down at NYU, the big expert, uses this technique for his patients. He tells them to think of it as a snapshot, proof that you're actually in one piece." When with morose triumph Shapes spotted the flaw—"But when I play it back I'll be hearing it above *ongoing* noise, so how convinced will I be?"—Templeton persisted: "Do you sing? The literature suggests singing may work even better."

At three in the morning, Shapes found a half-played tape in the well of the small Sony machine he kept around the house to amuse the grandgirls and took it to the coffee table in the living room. Sitting on the couch, he bent close.

"Tes—"

He remembered to wheel up the volume. "Testing." He honestly didn't know about this. Trying to cure yourself—wasn't it suicide's reverse lining, another symptom of laughable pride? If anything, an unmessy suicide seemed somehow easier to him than to sing alone into a tape recorder. Despite his reputation, he wasn't impetuous, the type of person who could be his own sole appreciator. The only truly rash thing he'd ever done in his life was at sixteen, when he and Sidney worked as the night cleaning crew of the RKO Tilyou. In the middle of the final show of the evening, shortly after arriving for work, Shapes convinced Sid to come back behind the screen with him, where they found chairs and a long table. Feet up, enjoying the two excellent full-sours they'd bought on Neptune Avenue for a later snack, they watched great skittish forms soak through the enormous canvas screen, mating, breaking, sliding. Shapes at one point put down his pickle and stood in order to see if he could keep step with the gigantic moving gestures on the screen. ("No problem! Only if there's light at my *back*," he whispered as Sid hissed *Sit down! Sit down!*) But the assistant manager, Shermie Miller, a lordosis case, was back there in no time at all, firing them both on the spot.

Ever since then, a reputation for carelessness. But undeserved. Perfectly-reasonable-at-the-time decisions, like selling to the Goolsbys, were viewed by others, Shapes knew, as follies: Anywhere I Hang Myself Is Home. The tape spool wound. While, like the shadows at the Tilyou, it was the reverse: it was Shapes's every *non-*touch that stung, he knew all too well. No barking at Elise to put down a second slice of pound cake. Never admitting to Telscher what a terrible idea (even if it was his own) he deep down knew an actual Sound Barn would be. Not once making it clear to Amy how hurt her refusal to let him love her left him. Never encouraging Bennett to have a little fun while there was still time.

"Testing, testing." Taking a deep breath, he sang:

OntopofoldSmokey . . . and shut off the machine. Started it again: "I'd like to confess to having hardly anything to confess, which I realize is a crime in and of itself." And then, to the previous melody, he sang: *Ithinkthisisstupid*, and again shut off the machine. In the dark his watch by then read 3:45. He'd never make it to morning sane. Sweat had broken out all over him. He rewound the tape, stopped it, and played:

FORCE IT BACK WHERE IT—the din of which nearly blew him from the room. He lowered the volume considerably.

—*from. If all of us are clear in our minds that we really want this done, I'll try to see what I can do. I'm sure we can at least agree that we have no collective desire for this particular cold front sweeping down from the Dakotas, so just give me a second here . . . All right—done. It's gone. Stalled. No more threat of snow for the time being. And while I'm at it, what about this little low moseying up from the Carolinas, which also could be pesky? I'm going to blow that away too.*

—This the tape, he realized, Monte Vee had originally sent of Iris on the air, when Shapes first was considering an ad.

Are you curious to know what you could have gotten if I hadn't interceded? A cold front would have continued driving down from the Dakotas and dropped a lot of icy air first on the Midwest—and around Thursday it would have been in our laps. And that low I took care of, off Carolina? That would have stalled offshore, probably somewhere around Delaware: and it, plus the cold front, would have given us . . . that's right! four, five, six inches minimum. At number 9 on the recorder's volume wheel, Shapes barely was able to hear himself. Iris on the other hand was coming off clearly and loudly at only number 3. *So what you want to know is what the weather's going to be after I took care of it for you. Okay. For starters: at three P.M. it was thirty-seven degrees and the wind is light at eight miles an* hour, gusting to fifteen, and the barometer is holding at thirty point six—and best of all, guys, there isn't any of that unspeakable stuff falling down. How 'bout them apples?

Iris—*what if Iris were God?* The rabbi at Telscher's synagogue said last month that when we're in the greatest pain, His back seems turned away. Headed where, hiding how, *masquerading in what other guise*—we don't know. When the peelings-back first began to happen to him, Shapes once or twice wondered if he himself wasn't being asked to shoulder the Part temporarily.

When he had next looked at his watch the time was five to five. And six hours later, in the office of the Barn, in front of (of all people) Al, Shapes lost consciousness completely.

Amy was back. "Still hasn't signed you out?"

"What did you learn about the bill?"

"I didn't think you were interested. Nothing. I have to call later this afternoon, after you're home. *If* you're home. Aren't you wearing your maskers?"

"Watch your back, sweetie: here comes this nice lady with my lunch."

Amy's mood was only partially improved when two hours later Shapes was discharged. Siegel, sending him on his way, had said, "I'll see you in the office next week. We'll go over the results of the tests together, but right here today I'd say Ménière's Syndrome. But we'll have to see all the findings." By that hour Amy was forced to fight out-rushing Manhattan traffic, and twice she tormented the car, bucking it in a confusion of gears, blamefully slapping at the steering wheel whenever she needed to downshift: "This damn car!"

Shapes was only getting what he deserved for having originally driven straight from the dealership to Amy's house the morning he had bought her the car some weeks ago, passing up a dozen service stations on the way that for a couple of bucks could have scraped off the invoice sticker. Mistake number two was parking it down the block: too stagey, making more of it than needed be. Bennett at the store, the kids at dance camp, Amy was alone in the house and had followed him down the street barefoot and tssking. She'd stared at it dully: "Very nice, you bought another Volvo," then looked at her watch. "I have to pick up the girls." She said nothing for awhile when Shapes held out the keys to her. Then:

"Are you *crazy?* Do you think we're rich? We couldn't even afford to get it fixed!"—studying the bald numbers on the invoice sticker, extra kindling for his pyre.

"Shift gently," he told her now, "it'll respond."

"Maybe yours does," Amy answered tightly. "Not this one." But once they were successfully out of the city she drove more smoothly. The wave swish in Shapes's ears from the maskers—two tiny FM transmitters, small as hearing aids, sending out a constant sea tone louder than the tinnitus—plus the depressants Siegel had prescribed lulled him into a broken sleep. He was alert enough when the time came to warn Amy off the Thruway an exit earlier than the usual one for Goshen (construction) and then through part of the detour. She seemed to be managing, and again Shapes closed his eyes.

"WHAT DO I DO HERE?"

He opened them. The car was stopped at a temporary traffic light placed above an ambiguous intersection. After a quick survey he advised, "Go left." When she made a sharp turn into a road perpendicular to the one he'd meant, he cried, "No, *there!*" turning around in his seat to point at the correct route receding in the distance.

"You said left."

"That *was* left."

"That was *straight*," Amy said.

"It wasn't—it angled off. Didn't you see it angling off?"

"THEN THAT'S NOT LEFT. ANGLING OFF IS STRAIGHT. IT CAN MAKE AS MANY CURVES AS IT

WANTS—IT'S STILL THE SAME ROAD, STRAIGHT AHEAD."

"I disagree."

"I know you—I KNOW YOU DO. AND YOU'RE WRONG."

"I can hear you, you don't have to scream."

"Do *I* know that? I have to assume . . . What an incredible *grouch*!"

"How we get back now is the question," said Shapes. "This road should . . . , I think it does—*what are you doing?*" Way over on the left she'd found an unsanctioned break in the divider and was beginning an appalling U-turn—the stationwagon suddenly straddling the passing lanes in both directions, a double target.

"I'M TURNING AROUND AND GOING BACK."

The pausing of his heart made the maskers sound even louder in Shapes's ears, bested by a chorus of shocked, dopplering horns on both sides. He shouted, "Don't ever do that again!—I've never seen anybody do a stupider thing!"

"Here's your wonderful 'left' again." They were back at the disputed intersection. "Just so I'm positive: *This* is the one you want?" When Shapes only grunted, Amy said, "Fine. We're taking it then. But all *I* have to say—"

"I *wish*," he muttered.

"—is that only someone who's not clear about giving directions, who doesn't quite know what 'left' and 'straight' means, could think that was *left*."

Shapes leaned over to the air-conditioning panel, turning it up: it was warm in the car. He asked her by way of a final word to please not speed. "This is too nice a car to wreck." Admittedly not the kindest thing to say, all things considered, yet still her reaction was a surprise: meek small nods with something gravitational to them.

Shapes strained against his shoulder belt for a closer look. "Crying? Why? Because of me? That business back there? Don't. What is it?" He reached to turn down, then altogether remove the right ear's masker. "It's everything lately, isn't it?"

He gave a sigh. "You better than anyone know the kind of life I had with Mom," pulling out the left ear's masker too. "And she with me. All marriages are intricate and terrifying, and *this* one . . . the humiliation, the guilt on both sides. But love—remember this—there was for a long time love also."

"And *you* never in all those years slept with anyone else?" Amy wailed. "YOU DON'T HAVE TO TELL ME." Tears were dropping now. She looked into her side mirror, as if at something that was trailing the stationwagon. "WHAT YOU SAW THAT AFTERNOON AT THE MOTEL . . ."

Shapes pushed at himself, trying to wring away the sensation of pressure caused by the removed maskers, to pop the ears into some clarity, understanding.

"BENNETT AND I HAVE HAD OUR PROBLEMS—"

"Is your window completely shut?"

"Oh, Daddy, don't pull this deaf stuff now!" Amy then must have squeezed the wheel, which the car translated into a veer—and three uncompassionate screams of a horn leapt from the blind spot to the stationwagon's right.

Shapes said, "Careful," once she'd straightened out again.

"YES, RIGHT, I DID IT ON PURPOSE! AND IT'S MY FAULT HE WAS GOING TO PASS ON THE RIGHT!"

"Sweetie—"

"The 'sweetie' who you're making pay and pay? You saw Merrit at the motel and you told Mommy—and she punished me too, right? But do I *care* about the money, hers or yours? I never wanted anything from both of you anyway!"

Motel? Merrit? What motel? Merrit was the fiddler in Ben's exquartet. Merrit?

"Just because a person falls in love? I don't think it's so taboo. I can accept it, I can make peace with it—but *you* can't. Bennett—"

Bennett? *Was she saying Merrit and Bennett . . . ?* With the hand cupping both miniature maskers Shapes undid his shoulder belt to begin sidling toward her.

"Don't bother—BOTHER ME, I'M DRIVING, I HAVE TO PAY ATTENTION. OTHERWISE I'LL SCREW UP AGAIN, RIGHT?"

9

"Are you Iris? I'm Amy Shapes." Amy took inventory of her. Freckles the size of Rice Krispies spread all over the white face. Chin too small. Big bosom. Narrow eyes.

"How's Charles doing today?" Iris asked.

"Oh, much much better. They're pretty sure now it is Ménière's Syndrome, and the maskers and sedatives they gave him in the meantime are letting him sleep." Immediately Amy hated herself for letting the report go any farther than the curtly upbeat "Great!" she'd decided on in the car coming over. "He hasn't slept for *so* long."

"No relaxation or imaging exercises, I'm sure," Iris said. "That would be too much to hope."

"No, no, yes, those too," Amy lied.

So long since she'd had a real rival, she was out of practice. It was like fording a stream on slick wet stones. But she needed to try. For instance she knew (because Bennett had mentioned it) that the woman had a deaf child—but no custody. "Our girls are a little under the weather. Just colds, nothing serious, but I thought for a change I'd let Bennett stay home with them and I'd come in. I should start learning the ropes anyway if my father's going to be out for any length of time."

With emphasis Iris said, "Wednesday is usually quite slow. Maybe you'd rather go back and keep Charles company."

But Amy went behind the counter: "Put my bag down here?" By its long, colorfully braided strap she picked up a red woven tote bag that had scratched against her ankle while she was pushing her old Coach onto a shelf below. "Is this Central American?"

Iris gave her a queer look. "It's one of those I make."

Amy held it up; compared to her own safelike purse, it lacked a bulge, it weighed hardly anything. "And sell them to stores?"

With an even more puzzled expression Iris said, "Two of them I gave to—"

Amy undid the wooden barrel-button that served as a clasp. "Lined too." (Inside were a white envelope, some keys, a cellophane slit-pack of tissues.) "And you're able to make this strap any length you want, by just tying it short or long?"

Iris stepped forward—"Yes"—and leaned to shove the bag back toward the floor, where Amy had discovered it.

"No, wait," Amy said, and then—"Oh I feel terrible"—as the shoulder strap, pulled in opposing directions by two grips, limply came apart like a piece of cardboard bent back one time too many.

Regarding the bag as though farther away from it than she was, Iris said, "That's all right." But Amy took pains to outdo her in reassurance: "I can fix this. With two kids in the house I do a lot of mending. If you tell me what kind and color wool you used . . ." Iris reached out and took the bag back, saying, "It isn't a problem."

"It's so unusual. I've never seen anything like it."

Again Iris looked at her oddly. "The three you have are identical"—coming around the counter and stuffing the damaged bag deep into a shelf out of harm's way, away from continued discussion. "I gave Bennett bags to give to you and your children." She went through the door, into the back office.

"*Are* those the same?" Amy was obliged to scramble. Bennett had been given bags? Why? *Were* there bags?—or had she just been maneuvered into acknowledging nonexistent bags, making her look like a fool?

After that Amy couldn't find a comfortable place for herself in the store. She could conceivably have ordered Iris out of the office (if she had had the nerve), saying that she had to get busy with the most important of her father's affairs; but the office was oppressive, it made her claustrophobic, white cardboard covering the small windows, the air-conditioning clattering but unable to clear the room of the sweat and fart smells of the sheets and pillowcase stacked to one side of the sleep sofa the Russian used.

He, Al (ugly ugly man, too short for that many muscles, and, just like Bennett said, walked like a monkey), was underfoot all the time, with as little to do as Amy. Iris, as the afternoon progressed, kept him semi-occupied: ripping up cartons in the stockroom, hosing down the front sidewalk, and even pulling up weeds from the concrete apron behind the building—while Amy herself tried to look busy by walking around the customerless selling floor. On one of her circlings, a cardboard display tub, printed with a bricklike pattern on the exterior sides, caught her attention. The tub was filled with six-packs of recording tapes. "Should we be keeping this thing here so close to the door?"

Iris was planted behind the counter and from somewhere had found yarn and was mending her bag. "A dump," she mumbled unclearly, red woolen streams running down past her chin.

"Well yes, but it doesn't have to stay that way," said Amy. "I think this, to start with, should definitely be moved. Someone casually dips a hand in, grabs a few of these tapes, and is out the door before anyone knows."

"That's the spot Charles himself placed it."

"It's got to be moved," Amy was firm.

"Do you want me to go get Al?"

"No need." Bending, Amy already had her arms wrapped around the octagonal carton, which she was forced to nudge inch by inch (an umbrellalike sign slotted into the rim made it difficult to lift the whole thing at once); she could feel the tongue-in-groove connections in the cardboard creak against her chest and loosen with every shove.

"The thing you're pushing, Amy, *that's* called the 'dump,'" Iris informed her with a fractional smirk. "Manufacturers give us one when they run a special—to save shelf space." She plucked a fiber off her tongue. "You sure you don't want Al to give you a hand?"

Now a difficulty, though. A cabinet filled with weighty stereo equipment was blocking progress. Amy gave this cabinet a small initial push—"Are these all plugged in?"—and yet one more. There was a small yielding. Then the cabinet began to teeter. Iris—as Amy dove at it, applying her breasts to it—didn't say a word.

When the cabinet was stilled, Amy walked it carefully by its corners, enough over so that the display barrel stood more or less free, in a central area midway in the aisle between the audio equipment and the portable televisions. That left only herself—to get her own body out of the aisle.

With a hip she tried moving one of the TV pedestals, but it turned out to be one long single permanent riser. She was trapped. One of the wall clocks (advertising a brand of Japanese speakers, and hard to decipher for all the cluttered lettering on its face) read 3:45. She'd never said anything about working the entire afternoon. Crouched from view, she called out, "Is that clock right?"

"I'll straighten everything back up," said Iris, "if you have to go." Two young boys, no more than ten or twelve years old, were entering the store, looking around.

"I told my father I'd stop by there around fourish. See how he's doing. The new medication and all." Reaching up, Amy with a yank pulled the whole dump down over on its side before rising and stepping around the mess of spilled-out tapes. In the doing she must have snagged her sweater-blouse; she was conscious of a long corkscrew of fiber bobbing ridiculously in time to the swing of her arms as she went toward the register and her purse. But she tried to resist embarrassment. Other than Bennett and Merrit, certain kinds of lax defeat had been her only reliable friends throughout the years. In college she had never studied. As a mother she bought cookbooks about nutrition and protein-complementary meals but instead slid overly expensive rib steaks and lamb chops under the broiler nearly every night. And with Merrit there'd been no difference: not the self-command sufficient to give him up before he did the giving up, to steer him into taking the girls and herself to England with him. (To love him hadn't taken any great control; to take *advantage* of the love and from it make herself happy, that would have.) "Have Al," she instructed Iris briskly, "clean all those tapes up. Or, if he can't, you do it. Thanks."

However Iris already was walking in the direction of the two wandering boys, one of whom wore a blue Yankees cap over the bald head of what was probably cancer treatment. "Can I help you, gentlemen?" It was at that moment that Al came out onto the floor—and with one look at him the two kids took off at a run, out of the store and to the bikes they'd dropped in front. In the scramble, the one with the baseball cap lost it for a second and had to get off the bike, retrieve the hat, and get back on with it before riding away.

"They steal?" Al called over to Amy.

Casually Iris strolled back to where she'd been mending her bag. "I doubt it." In the meantime, though, Al had rushed to the front door, broom in hand. Opening it, he shouted to the fast-pedaling kids:

"Hey Kojak! Who loves ya, babee!"

AUGUST

10

"Sit down," Sid urged. "Talk. Bennett drove him up there? It went okay?"

But Shapes left the room to go get the manila folder. Telscher pressed on when he returned:

"This Vogelsang fellow provides him with a place to stay, I assume. On the premises, like we did? Something more livable?"

"It's a cheese store, but you knew that. Above it is a large room that's used, I gather, for Vogelsang's church or whatever. That's where Vitaly sleeps, up there."

Telscher said, "Thinking about it, I just feel that he did finally appreciate and understand the situation. I'm sure you explained it to him very well—that we were overstaffed. Because the last thing I want is him feeling that *I*—"

"He went—that's all," and Shapes opened the folder.

Sid changed the subject. "I'm so busy with this *fokokte* politics I don't know what's doing with you. You aren't I see wearing the things in your ears. Which must mean the noise is getting a little bit better."

Shapes admitted to some improvement.

"And you use the radio at night like they told you—tuned between stations? Does that work?"

Innocent Sid believed in everything. "You try it yourself tonight. The error is fundamental. To add one noise to another noise doesn't necessarily result in a whole *other* noise—but two separate noises. And, if you add another, *three*. The noise of the radio static, the noise of my ears roaring, and worst of all the noise of my *thinking*. Thinking that I'm lying there purposely listening to a top-of-the-line Sony play static instead of Beethoven."

Telscher shook his head as Shapes went on: "Thinking about Beethoven, about *Beethoven* thinking—who also had to lie there at night, but without a radio. Deciding whether or not he was going to allow the whole business to be unbearable."

"But didn't, he didn't allow it," Sid said with heat. "If he'd given in, he wouldn't have written what he did."

"Sid, he was Beethoven."

"So you be Beethoven too!" Telscher stared dully, with the powerless annoyance of the well at the ill. "You make up your mind that you *can* deal with it. A person can change when he has to."

"Except," Shapes noted, "Russian cabdrivers. That my phone? Is the phone ringing?"

He left the room to take the call in the bedroom, with the door closed. "Hello?"

"Let me speak to Al. This is Howard Gelman."

Shapes said "Yes" neutrally.

"Well, are you getting Al?"

"He's not here, Rabbi."

"Then do you know where he is? HIAS and NYANA won't tell

me; Updegraff at Children's Services says he doesn't know; and of course now you won't tell me—none of you thinking I can manage to figure out where this new job you've stashed him in is. One of the females at your store already told me: the Woodstock area. A store. But what *kind* of store, Shapes? Don't if you don't want to tell me the name, just the kind of store it is. Another stereo store? Because you know I'll find it myself, find *him*, eventually. No matter what!"

"Calm down."

"You're right, I should be calm. I saw all this coming. Who told you you would ship him out? Who warned you? The man's a disaster—but you go ahead and take him from me anyway, who knew how to deal with him better than anyone."

"In what kind of way," Shapes asked, *"do* you know him?"

"Will you at least admit to Woodstock? The female in your store told me he's in Woodstock. The Woodstock area. That could mean Catskill, Dorchester, that could mean—"

"Rabbi, I'm sorry but I've got someone here with me and I have to get off."

"You should know that if I have to, I'll stop strangers on the street to find him. I just thought I'd first try being reasonable and hope you'd be reasonable. We could still be that. Maybe you want to call him first and tell him I have news about his daughter. You there, Mr. Shapes? This is very urgent."

Shapes had a brainstorm apropos of Nina, Vitaly's child. With an air of perfect innocence, he said to the rabbi: "His daughter Anna, you mean."

"He has only one. Of course, Anna."

Shapes said, "Why don't you tell the message to me. I'll see that Vitaly gets it."

"Why don't *you* cut out the crap and tell me where he is!"

"What's the message?"

"Sure, sure—and she might be dead by the time he finally hears."

Shapes's heart beat rapidly. "What is the message?"

"And in that case it won't be *my* fault for a change, he won't be angry at *me* for not telling him. It won't be me he'll beat up, ohnonono."

"*What is the message?*"—the only thing preventing Shapes from having an attack of palpitations being Gelman's hysteria, its superiority, indicating a bluff.

"I'm going to tell *you?*"

"If you call here again I'm phoning the police to file a complaint." Always Shapes was hanging up on this man. "Do you understand?" He put the phone down, and waited another few minutes, but no return call came.

If Sidney had overheard anything through the door, nothing was admitted to. He was sitting at the edge of his chair, in a renewedly eager posture. "I didn't mean before that you should *be* Beethoven. But since you're having this experience anyway—"

"What kind of 'experience'? It's a sickness, a syndrome."

"—and since it involves sounds in your head, you *use* it. Put it down in notes, make some music yourself, make something out of it."

Shapes tugged down at his cheeks in distress. "You're sounding like Iris. Music as some kind of bodily substance, cholesterol that clogs you up or that you mold with—Chopin hawking up the Ballades like phlegm globs. Please, Sidney." Shapes opened the folder. "This top sheet has the primary figures. If you'll take a look you'll see the problem. The one or two months when she first came—I'm speaking of Iris—were unusual, businesswise—"

Telscher's face was stony as he told Shapes he wasn't listening to any of this.

"—a blip on a graph, an oddity. But you see it then evens out again. The way I did the figures once more last night was to include those months at a rate of monthly loss the *same* as before she was hired." Shapes lifted yet another page from the folder. "And in that case the number I get is something on the order of—"

Sid in defiance sat deeper into Shapes's sofa. "I'm such a terrible guy? I did something *so* unforgiveable?"

"And I'm such a *schnorrer*," Shapes set down the sheets of figures, "that I'm expected to sit on this money I all of a sudden have and never pay back my biggest debt, give both of us our freedom? That's nicer?"

"Let *me* decide what my freedom is." Telscher ran a fingertip along an inch of the upholstery's welting. "The *timing*, Shayel. I'm supposed to believe it's just a coincidence that right after I convey to you what Amy came to me with—"

"No one's ever said the man's a candidate for a diplomatic career. And can you tell me for a *fact* that chemotherapy is as common in Russia as it is here? He saw a bald kid and he didn't know any better."

Telscher shook his head. "*Kojak*. Poor kid to begin with—and then to be mocked by an adult. But that was the minor thing. It was the other."

Shapes stared at the snake plants on the fireplace mantle; Doris, who came in now once a week to vacuum and clean for him, had run a rag down their sharp spears, something Shapes would never have thought to do. "I know my own daughter—what to give credence to and what not. Vitaly's a womankiller in only one definition of the word."

"I'm laughing, Charlie. But Amy was crying. He came on to her *and*, she says, to Iris. But she made me promise not to tell you."

"Exaggeration's been Amy's worst habit for as long as I can remember. For instance this: she and Bennett seem not to be having a good time of it at the moment—and recently she tells me that she saw Bennett going to a motel with his violinist."

Sid held up warding-off hands: "Should I hear this?"

You, whose frankfurter pokes in too far—why not? "I'm using it just as an example."

"Who is she, this violinist?"

"Not a she: a *man*. But don't you see?—it's Amy's desperate fantasy. Elise was the same way: when all the weight came back the second time and the alopecia, when she was losing hair—she also brought home stories about mashers among our friends, our neighbors. My point exactly." Telscher stiffened and began swearing he had never . . . "And not Vitaly with Amy either. And *certainly* not between him and Iris, who's a kind of nun now, away from all that completely."

Sid remained thunderstruck. "Elise said *me?* In all these years I never had an inkling from you . . ." Resting a hand over the crocodile on his shirt: "If I ever for a moment suspected that you even *possibly* thought *I* . . ."

Shapes let him hang there a little. "This Gelman character, who keeps bothering you with the calls? That was him just now."

"You believe me, don't you?"

"Of course I do. I told you, Elise was just making trouble."

"Like you are now," Telscher said with pique. "Which is why you brought it up." He got to his feet, pleased to have wrested away the advantage. "We'll talk another time."

Shapes motioned toward the figures in the manila folder. "I'm going ahead with this on Monday, talk or no talk."

Telscher let himself down at the sofa's edge. "But really—what about what Rabbi Gelman has been saying? He knows Vitaly very well."

"Or would like to." Shapes still wanted to think he'd simply heard the Russian wrongly that day in the D-Lux (*Suck my cock. Wants me to fuck him in the* . . .), the tinnitus, the air-conditioning, the furry gutterals of the accent all contributing to a misinterpretation. "Al never gave any trouble to me. Nor to Iris on her own. Only it seems to Amy and Bennett—to whom *everything* is a problem."

"You shipped him off to Vogelsang's, though. Why, if he's such an angel?"

Feeling bad enough, Shapes hated being called disingenuous too. "Pressure is pressure." Sid went a little pale around the mouth, and Shapes attempted to soften it. "Becoming auditor is important to you. It should be."

Looking down to his lap, Sid was shaking his head. "No change in fifty years. Everything you think gets said, no discretion, no biting your tongue." He reached over and pulled open the file folder he wanted nothing to do with before. "So let's talk. What price, bigshot?"

Shapes pushed his own fingers down on the file. "Iris does inventory, you know, and some—not all—of that is down here, what I can read of her writing. But when I walk around the stockroom, what's written here seems to me a little high. I don't see that much in stock or on the floor. I'm going to ask her to do another inventory this week, which maybe Amy can help her with. Otherwise, the sales and rental slips are straightforward. I have no problem in giving you the worth of what's there and then some—but for Bennett's sake, I'd ask you to walk through with him and do your own estimate."

Telscher looked at Shapes in shock. "You're giving Bennett the store?"

"Thinking about it."

"He *knows* you're giving it to him? You've discussed it?"

"He's involved in the day-to-day. And now that Amy wants to come in part-time—"

Telscher hit at the coffee table with two fingers: "No! The *last* thing he needs is an unsuccessful store. Let him go back to his career."

"His first violinist—the one he's supposed to have . . . he went to England to play in an orchestra. There is no career. Bennett needs something else."

"But this?"

"Is it Bennett that's uppermost on your mind—or that you can't handle the idea of me buying you out, of not being able to take care of me?"

With a groan Sid sat back.

"My failures and cockeyed projects, haven't they been your security, the little bird in the miner's helmet? Admit it."

Telscher declared "I'm hurt," yet a moment later he was slapping his knees, recovered. "Two can play Doctor Freud. You're annoyed at me because I'm less enamored of the Russian than you are. And that you yourself realized—although you blame me for it and Amy and the rabbi, anyone—that you *had* to send him away. Plus you've had a hard time with your ears."

"Don't forget my consuming guilt over Elise's blood money burning a hole in my money-market account."

"And we both know you sleep very little, not nearly enough. That takes its toll. *But*," Telscher pushed the manila folder away, "we're talking about your *children*—their lives, their futures. Don't play fast and loose."

"So speaks the auditor." Shapes was sorry it had to come to this—insult, manufactured hurt—yet there was hardly a punch Telscher wouldn't roll with. "The soul of probity."

Sid got to his feet. "I see you want a fight. But I'm sorry, I won't."

"And never would. How you always won—the Fisherman's Punishment. Forget a new inventory," said Shapes. "Right here and now I'll give you—partial payment—a hundred and seventy."

Telscher headed for the door. "If we're going to do it, we'll do it right. *In my boring auditor's way.* A full, complete, slow, third-party, independent inventory. For me. Then—*maybe*—we'll talk about it again. Maybe."

II

"Oh, look at this *face* he's making—like I said something bad about Israel, that I hated Israel, when I *love* Israel."

So different than the quiet Sound Barn for Vitaly: all this man Monte does in the cheese shop, whenever he's here, is talk. Never shuts up.

"All I said is that there's got to be something peculiar to citrus-growing climates. But"—and Monte peeled back his fingers—"southern California, Florida, Israel: very, very difficult to obtain a decent meal. I give them credit for trying to *copy* good food, but maybe they shouldn't even bother. Trace minerals in the soil, acid in the people's stomachs from the citrus and that affects the taste-buds—I don't know. Of course, then you look at the Arabs, who live in the same part of the world and eat much better—so it can't only be the soil or the climate."

Vitaly meanwhile lets the half wheel of Jarlsberg thud to the cutting board.

Sitting at one of the three cafe tables along the far wall of the shop, Monte jumps up:

"The amount of film you're using! Less! Less!—I'm not made of money, you could get away with half that." He sits back down. "Of course there are exceptions. When Hill Folk did the big tour in seventy-one, it included Tel Aviv . . . which, by the way, is something I've been meaning to ask you. You knew about Hill Folk in Russia, didn't you? We were hearing that the *Man-Demonium* album—that and jeans—were what everyone nagged Western people to bring them."

Vitaly shrugs in genuine ignorance.

"So one night we hire two cars and drivers and have them take us to Jerusalem, a joint that turns out to look like a cave: an Argentinian restaurant. Know the one I'm talking about? A guy is dressed up as a gaucho at the door, all the waiters are also gauchos, the cooks are stationed at a humongous open-fire pit right in the middle of the room. Beef and mutton and kidneys and sausages for the mixed grill—all they serve—carnage—meat and more meat cooked on skewer-swords sticking point-down into the coal beds, big white hilts standing straight up. Picture it, Veet: *crosses*, dozens of crosses, and we're what, five minutes away from the Via Dolorosa. Everyone but us speaking Hebrew. Fanfuckingtastic. We close the place down, drunk as shits on Argentinian wine; they have to kick us out. Of course the Folk, anywhere they went, were *the* great partyers. You ever planning on going back to Israel?"

Vitaly soberly wipes the slicer against his aproned thigh. "Better for us here. Very nervous people there," and applies the tip of the slicer to the midpoint of the cheese.

"One, they have cause. Two, you think here's better? You who almost get sent to Pinebreeze because you stand up and won't take grief from some hopped-up P.R.? I bring you news, my friend—people are nervous everywhere. Diet deficiencies to some degree, but also it must be more elemental, peculiar to the species, like rabbits or fox terriers. But I bet they're less antsy in Israel than in Russia. You think?"

"What means?"

"Jumpy. What you said: nervous."

Vitaly shakes his head. "People, Soviet Union, they live okay. Not so *ganzer* nervous."

"Like you're hurrying back."

"Another time maybe. They would allow—maybe I do."

"God, Al, I love you, you're priceless. Love you and love you. *So* full of shit. Are the folding chairs in place upstairs? All of them?"

Vitaly, soon after Monte left, hears what he thinks sounds like a small cough of thunder. He's done with portioning out the Jarlsberg. He also hears one or two cars arriving in the back parking lot. For all of them, every one of these store owners who come to the services, he has contempt. They call themselves priests, ministers, whatever, but all they are as far as he's concerned are worthless fairies—though most of them are married. But married to the kind of woman who marries fairies (the town is small and in half a week he's seen them): women who run fevers and need cold forehead cloths when they bleed, who play the recorder. Women who do not ask first before climbing on top, who carry more money than the man, who write poems to the Spring and tack them up inside their houses beside windows. They want to seem like sugar birds but are poisonous creatures actually, and you have to be careful of them, *and* their fairy-husbands. (Like Charlesshappes's daughter and son-in-law Benyamin: apologize apologize apologize but destroy at the same time. A real fairy like Howie at least does not also always apologize.)

Vitaly switches on the sealer, getting it warmed up before wrapping the cheese chunks. Careful to use less plastic film, he only touches each piece to the sealer; tomorrow he'll weigh and put price stickers on the chunks. The ones who *aren't* fairies, they are old—but, like Monte, don't care for the idea. The clothes they wear and how they talk: as if they were twenty, not sixty. Mistake. The only *likable* people are old people (or young people trying to act like old people), embarrassed that the end is now obviously soon going to happen to them but hasn't yet. This was on his father's face all the time, the look of someone eating a portion of cutlets he'd never be able to finish, taking food out of someone else's mouth. Ala never understood about his parents. Ala would not have liked Charles-shappes either.

More footsteps up the back stairs. Vitaly puts each chunk of cheese back into the main refrigerator case, on one of the low, non-display shelves. He is momentarily free now, until everyone arrives and is assembled upstairs. He goes to sit at the same cafe table Monte occupied before. Some customers unbelievably eat at these tables, which makes him sick: how they open their small cheese packages in public and pluck at the smelly insides with their hands. After running his fingertips across the table's marble top to be sure there was no slick, he takes from the back pocket of his pants the nice sheet of white paper reserved for this, unfolding it, setting it down. He clicks his pen and in Russian writes:

Dearest Ninochka,
Now I think I have our perfect place, where I am now: near the Grand Canyon. Each minute I think in my heart how much you would be amazed by it. Good schools are not far away. It would be the finest place for us of all the ones I have investigated around the country. No one would bother a Poppy and a daughter who were living here. There are very few people who live around here and for this reason the radio stations must be very powerful in order to cover the vast distances, as in Siberia. I am starting to have interviews. They like me very much and are impressed with my experience and intelligence and my independence—and I am probably going to secure an excellent job with them.

SHAPES MISTAKEN

First however I must stay here for a few more months. They want me to do an analysis of their system. If I do a good job (of course I will!!) then I officially will be given the position and you will join me . . .

A drop of sweat falls onto the paper and ink-fuzz grows around two words. At night upstairs he drips like a horse, hotter here than anywhere he's been: in Vienna, Rome, Beersheva, Brooklyn, Peekskill, the Sound Barn—so much sweat that he needs a glass nursing pump like the one used by Ala to pull herself dry before going to the polyclinic in the morning. And tonight, after all the fairies have heated it up, the room up there will be even worse. More footsteps on the back stairs, more arrivals. He folds the letter into his shirt pocket, hoping sweat won't ruin it.

Most of the fairy minister-men in the room stand near the long side table, commenting on the platters of food Fred, the cook from Monte's restaurant, is placing there. (Vitaly has eaten at this restaurant, Vee's—or sometimes they call it Abou Ben Adhem's—nearly every night since the transfer, but the food is not nearly as good as in Israel, no matter what Monte says; too much lemon in everything, especially in the different eggplant pastes, which also need more garlic.) Monte, from the back of the room, greets him shouting, "How about my ice, Veet?" Vitaly points to the metal tub beneath the longest of the food tables and hurries over to his cot, tucking the letter between the foam pad and metal frame. Some of the fairy men get drunk after the services—some priests!—and the cot, not far from and off to a side of the lectern, becomes attractive . . . but if one of them ever vomits on this, his only bed, he will strangle the pig. Quickly he reclines, raising himself on an elbow. The only good thing about being up front on the cot is that he's allowed to stare impolitely at the men; they are helpless to stop him. No Iris tonight yet. She told him he'd love it here at Monte's and he assumed he'd be living with her, not on some cot. When she *is* around, she looks at him as though she'd never fucked him, very innocent. But to tell the truth he is happier free of her.

Monte was approaching the lectern.

"Settle down, people." Silently he counts heads—"A *minyan*," he smiles—and the men sit down on the folding chairs and take up their books and papers. "So why don't we start. You guys'll recover from the heat but I'm less sure about my *babaganoujh*. My pad, babe?"

Vitaly's elbow is on it. He passes it over to Monte, who places it against the lectern.

"Alrightee everybody. Let's begin: '*Holy Father, Blessed Father, Kind Father*—'" The other men speak the words at the same time, reading from a sheet of paper tucked into their books. Slowly Monte brings his arms away from his sides, raising them, standing them out like wings:

"*Good Father, Speaking Father, Telling Father, Teaching Father, Father of Lessons, Father of Instructions*, we're here again, gathered in Your Presence, set to learn what it is You want us to do or think or feel." Monte's arms reach for the ceiling. The other standing men also put their arms straight up and Vitaly sees many many pairs of socks. Monte's arms come down. He looks out at the dozen or more fairies:

"Who wants to lead off?"

The man who owns the shoe store (who has a face like a cat's) raises his hand. "Celina is dancing tonight, so I'm probably going to have to leave before the service is over. Do you mind, Mont?"

"*Reverend*," Monte corrects. "All right, start." Turning to Vitaly: "My pad?"

Vitaly looks at him.

"Pad? *Pad*-yetye?"

"You have."

"Right"—slipping it out from under the book. "Okay, Michael first and only this once, brother. Our holy services are a little more important than Celina's performances." Clicking down his pen: "Ready? Hit it."

The shoe-store owner opens his book. *"And it shall come to pass, when—"*

"Whoa-whoa-whoa . . ."

"—when many evils and troubles are befallen them . . . How many is that?"

Monte writes on. The shoe-store owner looks to Vitaly, who stares back expressionless. Monte is counting, using the tip of his pen—"Fourteen. Close enough"—and calls for the next reader while the shoe-store man meekly works his way down the aisle and out of the room.

"Me," the man from the bicycle shop gets to his feet. He does what he did last week: book in one hand, balancing the spine, raising it until the pages flopped open. Not a bad little trick, something even Nina might like, but Vitaly doesn't smile because Monte won't. Monte never smiles during a service.

"So the man lieth down," the bicycle-store man reads, *"and riseth not; till the heavens be no more.* Don't bother counting, Reverend, it's fourteen—I keep track as I go." He looks around at the others with his terrible dead person's smile. Very ugly man. Especially in his tight shiny black bikeracing shorts, which make him look like pieces of wire wrapped together by electrical tape. "Get it all?"

Monte is writing rapidly. ". . . got . . . it. Sit down. Okay, someone else?"

The next to rise—with book already open—is the one who makes pottery in the neighboring store.

"Then he wrote a letter the second time . . ." The worst voice of all, high-pitched, ridiculous in a man, the voice more of a bad-tempered old woman screeching when someone sneaks in the queue in front of her. *"Saying, If ye be mine, and if, and if ye will hearken to my voice . . ."*

Copying, Monte yells, "Too many! That last stuff, the hearkening part, I'm leaving out. Fair's fair. Everyone in the vicinity of fourteen, fifteen words per congregant-witness. All right, now me."

Monte is the most entertaining chooser, at least to Vitaly, lifting his own book so the pages go riffling in a leftward direction, then stopping at one particular page. Then lifting the book even farther toward the ceiling, chin up and eyes shut, and the index finger of the other hand reaching up to rest atop the opened book. Then bringing the book down smoothly, the finger still in place, and giving the book a little shake as he returns it to the lectern. *"The breath of our nostrils, the anointed of the Lord was taken in their pits."* After he reads, he gets out the pad and writes down what he's read. But the man who sells the healthy foods (a store that smells even more like vomit than Monte's cheese shop) stands up and is ooh-ooh waving like a schoolchild who knows the answer. "I found something great. I'll be next!"

"You *found* something?" Monte eyes him. "That means you read it already?"

"Just running my eyes over it while you were transcribing your portion. That's allowable. I think that's allowable," the healthy-foods man appeals to the others. "Especially since it takes him twice the time—to read and then to copy."

"Okay, let's hear this *great*." Monte is finished writing.

"Well, I don't see it's cause to have an attitude . . ."

"You're holding up the service, Ray. Read it or don't, it's up to you, but if you have a complaint about how things are being run, bring it up before or after. Don't run this kind of number on us while we're in the middle like this."

The man, Ray, shrugs. *"Even the youths shall faint and be weary, and the . . ."*

The door, the one leading down the stairs along the back of the building, suddenly opens. Monte mutters "Someone's very late" and keeps on writing, but Vitaly bounds from the cot the minute he sees who it is. To get as close next to Monte as possible.

Monte finally turns. "Yes?"—at the same time the foolish bicycle man is standing up to call out: "Welcome!" But Howie Gelman says nothing. His hair is wet and matted down; it must have started to rain. He looks at Monte, and at the men in the chairs, and even at the food on the tables in the back—everywhere but directly at Vitaly. And doesn't say a word.

"Welcome," Monte calls. "Absolutely. It's an open congregation. Come join us in worship."

Howie's eyes widen. The pottery maker in the first row comes up to the lectern and pulls Monte aside—"IRS?"—but Monte pays no attention and goes on addressing Gelman: "We're open, nothing secret here. We're about in the middle, just, of our service. By all means have a seat."

Blocking the room's only exit, Howie only now looks specifically at Vitaly. Monte with flexing fingers is urging the pottery maker back to his chair. "We'll continue on. Who'll be next?"

A man with missing fingers on one hand and a missing foot was getting up (Vitaly didn't know which business he owned in town, but the man reminded him of Niki from the Institute, a Hero: same kind of crutch, same pinned pant leg). And someone else, the man who sells pajamas from India to wear even during the day in the street, says, "After him, me."

Yet Howie all this time continues to stare. Half-hiding behind Monte, Vitaly tries to stare back but sees how confused Howie looks, fuddled. Which is not bad, because if it comes to that, the move Vitaly eventually will make—a run for the door, knocking Howie down before he can get out the gun he is probably carrying—may work. Except that suddenly Howie turns around, reopens the door, and leaves through it, never having said a word.

The fairies excitedly talk all at once, but Monte says, "Let's *please* just finish up!" The Niki man, leaning on his crutch, is taking up pages of his book, bunches at a time, and flipping past them as though he knew what he wanted to find. Unfortunately the pages make a noise, just when Vitaly would instead like to be hearing the sound of Howie's feet clopping down the steps, the direction they take once they reach the parking lot. The crutch man stops turning pages. "*For they also built them high places, and images, and groves*—one two three four five six seven eight . . ."

"I'll tell you if you're short," Monte says. "Just go *on*." The crutch man says that's all the spirit wanted read, and he balances himself, preparing to sit.

The pajama-store man is already on his feet: "I can go a little longer, Mont." Monte, glancing at the door, finishes writing. "Go over," he whispers to Vitaly, "and see if that guy's still hanging around." He returns to the pajama man: "You by now should know that if one congregant is or isn't moved to complete his passage, that's the Mystery working and we don't interfere." Pajamas however is already lifting his book over his head, lowering it to rest a moment *on* his head, and carefully taking his hands away to balance it there a second. The book is taken down and pulled open.

"*Oh hear me now, O ye governors of the inhabitants of Bethulia: for your words that ye have spoken—*"

Monte wails, "Slower!"

"*. . . that ye have spoken . . .* (You ready?) *. . . before the people this day are not right, touching this oath which ye made and pronounced before God and you . . .*"

The healthy-foods man protests—"Way over!"—but Monte, stopping occasionally to look at the door, writes it all down. "It's all right, Stan, just this one time. All right, good, we're done. Now, everyone: Come Forth."

The men leave their chairs and form a semicircle in front of the lectern.

"AND IT SHALL COME TO PASS, WHEN MANY EVILS AND TROUBLES ARE BEFALLEN THEM SO THE MAN LIETH DOWN AND RISETH NOT TILL THE HEAVENS BE NO MORE THEN HE WROTE A LETTER . . ."

Monte stops and turns to Vitaly:

"You're the sexton. Open the door. If he's still out there, invite him in for the Revelation. Tell him it's the high point. Go on."

Vitaly goes nowhere.

Monte shakes his head and resumes reading. "THE SECOND TIME SAYING IF YE BE MINE THE BREATH OF OUR NOSTRILS THE ANOINTED OF THE LORD WAS TAKEN IN THEIR PITS EVEN THE YOUTHS SHALL FAINT AND BE WEARY AND THE YOUNG MEN SHALL UTTERLY FALL FOR THEY ALSO BUILT THEM HIGH PLACES AND IMAGES AND GROVES HEAR ME NOW O YE GOVERNORS OF THE INHABITANTS OF BETHULIA FOR YOUR WORDS THAT YE HAVE SPOKEN BEFORE THE PEOPLE THIS DAY ARE NOT RIGHT TOUCHING THIS OATH WHICH YE MADE AND PRONOUNCED BEFORE GOD AND YOU. You may be seated—except Ralph if he likes, since we're going to have to get up one more time." But even the one-legged man returns to his seat with the others.

Monte looks again toward the door. "Is he local? I don't recall the face. Maybe this once we'll skip reading it aloud a second time before we begin our study."

Up the bicycle-store owner pops. "I don't see why."

"The Revelation tonight," Monte pays no attention, "gives us, in my interpretation, the way *I* read it, a real vote of confidence. NOT TILL THE HEAVENS BE NO MORE THEN HE WROTE A LETTER. That could mean that the Supreme Power wants us to know that He *needs* to send these transmitted messages to us—as much as we have to read, record, and think about them. What I take from here is that it's saying that if He *didn't* reveal them to us now, He'd have to wait till the heavens disappeared, which probably would be never."

The pajama man rises, shaking his head. "I see that passage differently. It's saying what the heavens *are*. It's saying that the heavens are no more than a letter the Supreme Being writes to us. Which means—now follow me—that the skies, if we just choose to read them, are *saying* something. It's a vote of confidence, that's true—but specifically in *astrology*. Which as you all know I'm heavy into."

Monte consults the pad. "It's not tee aitch ay en: *Than*. It's tee aitch *ee* en: *Then*. *After* something, not *because* of something!"

Pajamas says not necessarily.

"Of course *necessarily*!" Monte glowers at Vitaly, still standing close to him like a dog: "Will you please sit *down*! Of course 'necessarily.' David, you read it to us—it was *then*, right? Like 'furthermore.'"

In his old lady voice the pottery maker apologizes to pajamas: "He's right."

"Well, I didn't realize we were being that strict and authoritarian," pajamas says. "Ex*cuse* me." And sits.

Monte checks his watch. "We probably also could quickly take this as a second theme, concentrating on the words *mine* and *pits*. Anyone see the article in the Sunday magazine section a couple of weeks ago about the coal miner? Young guy about thirty who tried it but couldn't hack it after about two weeks, it was that strenuous and scary? Great article; you ought to read it. Well, using that metaphor, this week's could be saying that that's what we're about here too, delving into the Revelations. It's rough hard work. It's like mining in a way." He pauses, taking another look at his watch, the door, the pad. "I guess those two are the major points of this week's Dictation. We can probably close now."

Up the bicyclist jumps one more time. "Toward the end—about it not being right to be touching the oath that's pronounced before us? Aren't *you* touching it, Monte, right now? Well, aren't you?"

"The *pad* you mean?" Monte looks exasperated, but immediately rests the pad against the lectern.

The bicyclist turns toward the other men. "Maybe at future meetings—"

"Services!" Monte cries.

"—we could have it up on some kind of altar once it's transcribed. We all could go up *to* it, read *from* it, but not actually be *touching* it."

"Good suggestion. Now we'll—"

"Because if we want to be taken seriously—"

"Everything here *is* serious!" Monte's face becomes red, he is beginning to sweat. To Vitaly: "Are you ever going to go out there and see what that guy *wanted?*"—and to the other men: "It's the Revealed Word—what's unserious about that?!"

"Because if one thing is literal, everything's got to be," the bicyclist goes on calmly. "We have to safeguard that—*even* if it means that we revolve the High Priestly duties so none of us gets lazy . . ."

"That's *fine*! Are you done?" After starting to pace, Monte abruptly flings himself back to the lectern. "What about this part: that talks about *the young men utterly failing*, Barry?" He raises his glasses onto his scalp's hair wisps. "*Groves and high places*—you tell me what *that* means, Barry! High places maybe refers to getting ahead of yourself? Ambitiousness? Bullshit grasping and striving?"

The bicyclist stares intensely at Monte, who however keeps going:

"And this reference here, to *images?* When Iris Seavy offered to make us a tapestry for the sanctuary here (and *some people* really had a hard-on for the idea because Iris is such a great craftsperson and all) well, if you remember—*if* you remember—*I* was against it. I didn't think there ought to be decorations in the sanctuary. And what comes up right here?"—Monte snaps all the fingernails on one hand against the pad resting on the lectern. "Exactly that! No *images*, or high places or groves.

"For God's sakes," he turns to Vitaly at his elbow. "Are you going out there and see what that fucking guy *wanted*!"

12

While Bennett was applying a manufacturer's decal to a corner of the window, Amy came out onto the selling floor to ask if he was expecting a delivery. A kid and a van?

It wasn't anyone Bennett had seen before, although the van was familiar—it brought small individual orders too small for the other, larger truck to bother with. When the kid handing over the lading slip and single carton said, "I wasn't sure whether it was to here or to the warehouse," Bennett said, "This *is* the warehouse" (and, signing the clipboard, got back from the kid a puzzled, whatever-you-say look).

Bennett peeled down the plastic invoice-jacket on the spot, but once he saw what it was he quickly let the whole thing be, setting the carton down in a corner and leaving it there.

The transmitter—Iris's transmitter—something he hadn't thought about in weeks.

Now it made the rest of the day unbearable, a potentially good day ruined. Good because it was Tuesday, Iris's day off. Amy and Iris—catastrophically—were becoming, if not friends, then at least confidantes. Amy lapped up Iris's stories of an unfortunate life—about her couldn't-care-less car-dealer mother out West, about co-owning a house with her mentally fragile brother Polk; about Polk's love affair and break-up with an Anglican priest currently in hiding from an accusation of embezzling part of an old woman's small fortune—and repeated them in bed at night to Bennett in superficial tones of disapproval, beneath which Bennett couldn't miss the touch of obvious envy of so eventful a life.

But all this was murder on Bennett, whose fantasies about Iris were steadily disintegrating. All he'd ever wanted was her cunt (and maybe only for a moment when he'd bent down and caught the fruit odor coming off her calves), but it seemed increasingly unlikely that he'd ever get it. He'd wanted, more exactly, for her to *offer* her cunt to him so that he could turn it down and then to be able to gnaw on the regret. The idea was part of his private stash of fantasy, like the woven bags for Amy and the kids, the seersucker jacket with its diagonal grease stain, the red tin snake.

The tin snake especially. "*Potent.*" Not a day passed that he didn't want to return it to her; not a day when he didn't turn over in his mind her message with it—*potent*—mocking him, mocking his doing absolutely nothing about it, about her.

After closing the store he drove home with Amy, having already decided exactly where on the route (close to home—too close for Amy to protest) to do what he now had to do. Bennett reached the spot (passing by the bakery outlet next to the water tower) and lifted his hand off the wheel to smack at his forehead. "What's today?"

Amy said it was Tuesday.

"Tell me it's not the eighteenth."

"It is the eighteenth. A problem?"

"I promised to donate some merchandise for a charity auction at a church in Ursulla. A couple of tape decks—good advertising for the store. But I was supposed to drop them off there in the afternoon, and forgot totally about it."

"Well, drop me off first," Amy requested, "because we're almost home. I assume the auction's at night? You'll have plenty of time to go back to the store and drive it up there. Which church is it?"

"*Damn!*" said Bennett.

For months he'd known the address by heart (long ago looking it up in Charlie's personnel ledger): Picaswee Road in Menyker, south of Woodstock—and he was able to imagine it vividly: a hippie-ish shack complex, or maybe a farmhouse. This was why, in the seven o'clock haze, after pulling off the road and riding down a wide winding drive and past a professionally painted sign:

REVEALED FAITH SCHOOL
For the Sensorily Disadvantaged

he was confused. The large caramel-colored A-frame building he stopped the Rabbit before was unexpected, and even more surprising were the grounds: stone paths with gaslights turning down a meticulous slope terraced at different spots with small pools and groves of young trees. Bennett got out of the car and walked around back to let loose the carton containing the transmitter, placing it momentarily on the ground. No other cars or people were in view. He'd already removed the tin snake from the tire well (it had been stuffed down into one of the woven bags and wrapped in turn inside his soiled jacket), had taken everything out together and then separated it all. If Iris wasn't home he'd put everything right at her doorstep: transmitter, snake, bags, jacket, and get out of there fast.

Suddenly he was being hailed, though, from some ways down the slope, a hundred or more yards: *"Yeah? Who is that?"*

It seemed to Bennett (who slipped the tin snake into a pocket of the seersucker jacket) that the caller was naked: a man, standing at the far side of a small reflecting pool, shading his eyes with the edge of one hand. Bennett in response put on the rumpled jacket, while the man now left the pool, climbing the path.

He wasn't in fact naked, only in very brief tan shorts, nothing else. And it was Polk, Iris's brother—Bennett recognized him from the museum, and his voice as well from that one time on the phone when he'd called the store. Approaching, walking up the grade, he was pinching at his breastbone as though the skin were a polo shirt. "Something I can do for you?"

Bennett bent and took the carton up into his arms. "I—"

Polk was giving Bennett the once over. "Looksee, if it isn't you, huh! I remember the jacket. You're not roasting in it?" He glanced over at the Rabbit some yards away. "Isn't she with you now?"

Bennett replied that he thought Iris might be here. Was she?

"Hardly." Polk sat on a bench stationed at the head of the path, the sort of advertisement bench found at bus stops, this one reading: *Meg Seavy Cadillac Olds Ask Your Friends—They've Bought From Us.* Sharper-skulled than Bennett remembered, like a piece of just-planed pine, Polk looked vaguely ill, although it may have been the lack of clothing.

"I have something of hers. A piece of equipment."

Polk stood up, slapping at his knees: "The old keys then. This way: they're in the house." When Bennett hesitated to follow: "Well, come *on*, and take that with you," gesturing at the carton. "You can leave it for a moment up near the house. Believe me, it'll be safe. I'm as honorary and honorable as the Swiss Guard here."

As they entered the large main room of the A-frame, immediately inside the door, Polk asked Bennett to ignore the walls. "I know they're disgusting." The room contained little furniture: a trestle table, two high-legged director chairs, a few empty pedestals. "I promised Iris I'll wash them—but not in this heat. Please take off that *jacket*."

Looking around it as though he, and not Bennett, was the first-time visitor, Polk remained standing in the center of the room. "You've just now learned something, though, haven't you? A-frames this high can't even *be* air-conditioned—and that loft up there by this time of the year figures to be six or seven degrees *hotter*. Yet you people intend to keep *children* in here year round?" He shook his head. From a wooden bowl resting on the trestle table he grabbed a ring of keys and inspected them closely, looking for a particular one. "I'm coming, be patient."

To avoid a jam at the front door, Bennett had taken a few further steps inside. The house was stifling, truly. Polk had pocketed the ring of keys: "But look, I don't ever lift. You'll have to do like the Cossack does and lift yourself. Don't you want to leave the precious jacket here?"

"I'm fine."

Polk regarded him. "I'm still a *little* surprised, I will admit. From what she has to say about you, I didn't put you down for the type."

"Who says about me? Iris says about me?" To buffer the eagerness in his voice, Bennett took off the jacket as a gesture of good faith and laid it on the floor in a crumple. "What type is that?"

"The Ted-type."

"Which is what?"

"Doesn't really know what's going on. *Pretends* not to know. Iris says I had a crush on Ted, but I know this nevertheless: if good old Teddy Ullivan can turn out to be a devil, so can anyone." Polk walked by Bennett, toward the front door, then unexpectedly slid down the door jamb and sank slowly to the floor, head back and legs out:

"Even *you*. Of course, she'd never tell you about Ted. Too many similarities. His father was backing him too, but his father owned the Sunapee, that big New Hampshire resort."

(To tower over Polk was awkward, and Bennett wasn't sure whether or not to sit. Or where. Instead he began to transfer weight from one leg to another, shifting like that until a cramp gathered in his left calf.)

"Monte's people worked all the Sunapee's workshops and retreats: Iris and her table of New Age vitamins. That's how they met, I assume. Took a walk on the golf course, Ted told her his troubles, they smoked some joints, did some fuckeewuckee—the next thing we know Iris is in *Puerto Rico*, managing an inn Ted's father also owned."

(Bennett reached down to his calf.)

"She was scuba diving and spearfishing and learning to haggle with provisioners and 'apprenticing' in that *santería* voodoo down there—but of course that was all front: she was busier setting up a studio at the inn for bootlegging rock-music tapes Monte was going to distribute. *That wasn't* in her postcards to me in Sheppard-Pratt. I also don't know how Ted first found out about it. But of all people to write to, he writes to me, stuck in bedlam!"

Polk put his palms flat to the floor, beside his thighs. "I called Rick, Iris's ex. That's why she's ruining me now. Revenge. I'll pay and pay forever—because I'm sure Rick was the one who blew the whistle on her. Ted's father had paid to keep it local—no federal tax agents immediately—but Rick in the meantime took his best shot and had no trouble getting sole custody of Timmy. You're fidgeting. Bored?"

"A leg cramp—finish your story."

"Story? No story." Polk slid upward against the doorframe. "Finished." He stood and beckoned Bennett out of the house, back to the carton.

Bennett hefted it up again. "This is something Iris ordered. It came—"

But Polk held up a hand. "I do better knowing *nada*." He led Bennett twenty yards to the right, to a storage shed, a replica in miniature of the A-framed house. On the door were three separate padlocks. Polk was slapping at his shorts: "Didn't I just have them? I put them in my pocket—they fall out? Look, rest that against the railing while I go back for them."

Bennett did set the carton down, but tagged closely behind Polk too. "What does bootlegging of rock tapes entail?"

Distractedly Polk replied, "Is she that great a lay?" searching the floor near the door.

Said Bennett: "I'm married." Meaning . . .—meaning what?

"I came over here, took the keys out of the bowl, put them in my . . . *here* they are! That's nice, to be married is nice. I was married to Larry, who's now away on an escapade and will probably come back to find me in the bin again. I hope, though, you're not married to someone who thinks she's very smart. A terrible thing. On a certain common level Larry is smart, not *deep*-smart but more like opportunist-smart, fools people into thinking he's knowledgeable because he's able to pitch himself a little higher than present company. That's usually not so hard; I can do it too—yet still I was 'the moron.' We were at a dinner party with Tony and Dallas and the Regensteins and they were all talking about Italian history and he kept using the word *Risorgimento* and I asked what that was. I vaguely knew. He says resurgence. But, come on, please!—I *knew* the English equivalent, I wanted to know what it *was*, the concept!—and the fact was *he* didn't know. So instead he stabs me in the heart. It's my fault he can't explain it to me: *For a Williams man you're an awful moron*, laughing and everybody else is laughing and even *I'm* laughing. Keys? Keys: right here in your hand, Polky. Tell me your name again?"

Walking the few yards back to the shed, Polk went on: "You probably don't even believe in devils. Larry doesn't. If he did, they'd send him to a rest retreat for disturbed clergy on the South Carolina coast, where he was during his famous *crisis of faith*, poor baby. But *I* know there are. No matter what Dr. Franziska helped me to see last time I was in the bin—that it's just my paranoia—I know they exist. Anyway, even if it *was* my paranoia and say it's *not* true that Iris is a devil and purposely crashed the car and paralyzed Rick and then has me hospitalized so she can have the house all to herself and be able to start the school in time to regain custody of Timmy before Rick moves to San Diego—say that's all true. Does that mean devils don't exist? The Chief's not paranoid—he's one of my artists, *was* one of my artists—and *he* knows they're around. All his pieces are protections against haints. If you went down to his house on East Anderson in Savannah and saw how many there are down there, all over the fences and nailed to walls and to the outside of the house and the garage and the little shed he works on, and over doors!" Polk had stepped up onto the deck of the shed; he undid the various locks. He peered inside: "Crowded. It may have to go on top of something else, but at least first try the floor. Maybe there's room. Push it in with your foot."

As Bennett ducked inside, Polk came in right behind. "Anything? Look right there, see if it'll fit in that corner." Bennett's eyes slowly were adjusting to the dimness. A full-sized carousel horse was stored to the right of the door; Polk put the ring of keys over one of its ears. Otherwise the shed was crammed with boxes, cartons of equipment—Audiobrights, Valsalvas, Cranmer-Lutzs, Woeneckes; speakers, tuners, and decks stacked one and two and three high. Vent slits in the ceiling did little against the limp sour odor of cardboard.

Polk's bare foot shoved at a box. "Even more room now." He turned the ring of keys on the horse's ear. "But you should have seen it yesterday. *Impossible* in here."

"Some of this seems . . ." Bennett began—but hit his head on a beam when he tried straightening up.

"Watch that."

"... like it's invoiced to our store"—and again Bennett lightly struck the back of his head.

Polk suggested they both back out. "There'd be more, but luckily they came out and took a lot away yesterday, Monte and this new guy of his." Polk was shutting the door and snapping the Yale locks.

"I'd like the keys," Bennett said, "I want back in"—but already Polk had covered his mouth in delight. "*Oh shit!* You're my witness. We were talking and I left them inside. The precious keys! Was there ever such a bad bad boy?"

"There isn't another set somewhere?"

"Me be trusted with *two* sets?" Polk turned to head back giddily to the house.

"Look, I mean it. That's *our* merchandise. I don't know what it's doing . . . but everything *really* has to be out of there!"

"Then why were you delivering?" Polk ran up the steps of the main house and was inside for only a flash before reemerging with Bennett's jacket dangling from his index finger. "This is the best I can manage on returns to you at the moment. Sorry. And listen—I'm counting on you to really tell them that I didn't lock the keys in there on purpose. Honestly. If they think that, which they will, it'll mean an extra six months in Sheppard-Pratt. What's so heavy in here—a gun?" Even as Bennett reached for it, Polk's fingers continued to investigate the pocket with the bulge. "My snake! My Meneny!"

Bracing himself with one foot on the second deck step, Bennett got hold of the jacket and with a clean snap regained the whole thing. "I was returning something to Iris," trying to stuff the piece of metal back into the pocket.

"You were to Iris, hell—you give it to *me*!"

Polk's sob, his overly bright eyes, and that previous question about a gun made Bennett more than simply nervous. Why mention something like a *gun*? Fishing hastily in his pants pocket for his car keys, he headed toward the Rabbit.

But Polk was right behind. "She gave it to *you*? That's mine! There are no devils? no demons?—fuck you, Doctor Franziska! *You just give that to me.*"

Then Polk abruptly reversed himself and again was running toward the house.

Bennett got in the car, locking every door. The carburetor sputtered, of two minds about catching; any harder pedal was sure to flood it. Bennett tried leaning around to roll up all the windows as Polk reappeared at a run.

"And these!"

Polk's hands were wrapped around not a gun but two chunks of granite weighty enough to have made him stumble twice on the way. "These too: why not take *them* away as presents too, clean me out entirely, all traces that I existed, the nerve I had to exist! I'm no dealer anymore, I'm a warehouseman—and next week I'll be back in the nuthouse!"

On closer view the big stones were pear-shaped sculptures of birds, of owls. If dropped on the car's hood, one of them could have killed the Rabbit for sure—and if the other were thrown through the windshield, onto Bennett's lap . . . What choice did he have therefore? He opened the window and pushed out the tin snake.

As it fell to the ground, Polk at first looked alarmed. But he put down the stone owls long enough to grab it. Quickly Bennett shut his driver's-side window as the engine at long last caught.

13

In June Shapes would have guessed he'd never see the woman again, but he couldn't have been more wrong. Judge Leona had turned out to be everywhere, into nearly everything, during the past few weeks. Arriving at the cheese shop the night of the problem, she'd worn optimistic green, a pants suit of a brightness that contrasted especially with Vitaly, gray and hapless, handcuffed to the wire apron of one of the cheese shop's cafe tables, looking numb and injured, as though the world had come to an end two days before and he hadn't been told. Leona quickly had one of the village cops undo him (the other, who'd answered the original call, had already gone to the hospital to have the rabbi seen to) and she stayed good-humored and calm—as opposed to Monte Vogelsang, who was hopping here and there with his precious piece of paper:

"The signatures of everyone! I got everybody out of bed and no one refused. Right here, plain as day: Al was our sexton, he was with us from start to finish, the whole service, during which this asswipe barges in on us, disturbs our worship, acts very very strange, says nothing like who he is and what he's here for, just stands there—then leaves!"

Then Monte would walk over to someone else. "And look down here where it says we all absolutely vouch for Al's character—see that?—that he's done the best job of anyone we've had as usher or sexton. So weird, this guy—not a word why he was bursting in on us, running this stare number on Al, really *drilling* him." And for the tenth time gesturing at ashen Vitaly: "Will someone other than me please go and talk to the man and tell him he's *not* going to be deported? I thought, big shot, you *loved* the Soviet Union and hate everything here? Man, the way he badmouths the Woodstock area. Vicious!"

It was Vogelsang who'd originally telephoned Shapes, urging Vitaly to speak also. From the Russian Shapes gathered the basic story. After Monte's church service, held in a room above the store, after this service and not able to sleep, Al had gone down to the cheese store to take care of some unfinished chores. While he was down there, Rabbi Gelman, who'd shown up earlier at the service but then left, returned—knocking on the back door. Vitaly, assuming it was Monte, let him in. Gelman insisted that Vitaly leave with him that night for Philadelphia, where he had jobs arranged and waiting for them both at the library of Temple University. When Vitaly said he wouldn't, Gelman picked up a cheese cutter and asked Vitaly, in that case, to stab him with it. Turned down again, Gelman started slicing into himself with the taut wire of the cheese cutter—into his forearm—shouting all the while that he was being murdered. The noise eventually brought the local police, who called Monte, who in turn called Shapes.

But once he hung up after that first phone conversation, Shapes was at a complete loss what to do. Some kind of intervention was needed, semi-official would be best, but of course Sidney was certainly the last one to ask. Then he'd had an idea.

Shapes himself heard the gristle of discomfort in his voice, to be phoning her this late, this urgently—yet Leona seemed not only to be up but as if she'd been half-expecting him to call on some matter or other. No long or meticulous explanations were required; she only wanted to know again which town it was, then suggested Shapes get up to East Dorchester quickly and she'd meet him there.

Thirty or so minutes after Shapes arrived at the cheese shop, Leona entered, in green, and with her a thin older man in a blue police windbreaker: the county sheriff. With the simple kindness you'd show to an upset child, the sheriff explained that there was nothing to worry about: no charges were going to be pressed against anyone for anything, and he was sorry about the handcuffs. Vitaly should stop trembling, put it all behind him, and make believe that nothing out of the ordinary had happened that night. During this Leona stood not far from Shapes, although at one point she went over to confer with Monte Vee. As the sheriff made ready to leave, she mentioned to Shapes that now might be a good time, until things settled down, to take Vitaly back to Goshen.

The great surprise was that she came along too—in Shapes's car (the sheriff had given her a ride up). Only slightly less startling was that all three of them—the Russian, the judge, and Shapes—were met inside Shapes's condo by Bennett, Sid, and Dorie (in her nightgown and robe). For some reason Bennett had come by. Not finding Shapes at home at that late hour—and not having a key—he had roused the Telschers with fears of something dire behind the locked door.

The six of them stood dumbly together in the foyer, at first too confused to speak. Sid and Doris proved easiest to get rid of (Sid couldn't look the Russian in the face); but Bennett wouldn't be swept out, making as if neither Judge Leona nor Vitaly existed. Shapes finally had to go with him into the bedroom and close the door.

"Some inventory person," Bennett said.

"He never did inventory. What's going on? Why are you here?"

"I'm talking about Iris. She's been picking you clean."

"I've kept track," Shapes fibbed. "I factored in the occasional item. It happens in retail."

"Have you? See 'occasional.' Go up to her house."

"What's this about? Was she in the act of taking something? What were you doing at her house?"

"She asked me . . ." Bennett paused. "A favor. To get a transmitter for her own use, off the books. A while ago. It finally arrived and I went out to give it to her and she was going to give me a personal check for it. But only her brother was there."

"We could have placed a special order."

Bennett said exasperatedly: "She asked me to keep it *off*."

"And the check?"

"A whole shed full of big-ticket items up there, apparently another place too for storage of more of them—and you're worried about her check?" He pointed beyond the closed door, whether to Vitaly or to Leona wasn't clear. "Your pal out there has been in on it too."

"I can't see how you managed to move a big transmitter out there by yourself."

"No, it's for hearing tests, it's small, something to do with her son and his school . . . what does it *matter* what it was!"

"I'm not completely following. I wasn't supposed to know about this when she first asked you? Why was that?"

Bennett paced, stopping once to tug sulkily on a tassled shade-pull at one window. "I didn't tell you. I should have."

"I'm just curious. And are you positive I need to know *now*?"

"You're just going to let her steal."

"I'll take care of it—but you're positive it was our merchandise?"

In despair Bennett looked at the ceiling.

"I'll see to it, I promise. If it still was solely my store and Sidney's, and the pilferage was insignificant—small things and very occasionally . . . The main thing now though is that what she's taking is *yours*."

Bennett's finger was an angry lance. "*That* hasn't been settled. We haven't given you a definite yes or no. Probably it'll be no."

Implying *stupidity*—that Bennett had somehow managed to help Iris steal from himself—was not the approach. "I'll speak to her."

"*Speak?*"

"It'll be taken care of."

Yet for all his agitation, Bennett then settled, as Sidney had, for a bare and vague explanation of what Vitaly and Leona were doing in the living room: *Some trouble in Woodstock*, Shapes told him. *Nothing that our friend needs to be near*. Stepping out of the bedroom and coming face to face with the Russian and the judge, wordlessly seated on sofas opposite each other, Bennett passed them by without acknowledgment, leaving the condo silently, too enraptured by his complaint to notice much.

"My son-in-law—" Shapes began to Leona, but she interrupted: was the bathroom that way?

When she left Shapes seated himself across from the Russian. "Why not try to go to sleep, Al—I can see you're very tired. My grandchildren use the couch when they visit overnight, it folds out. I'll go get you sheets." At the linen closet, just to the left of the bathroom door, while he removed a sheet and pillow and light waffle-weave blanket, Shapes could hear rushing water: not the toilet and not the sink, but the shower.

Vitaly accepted the fresh linens, cradling them pitifully in his arms. Shapes sat on an edge of the coffee table to again deliver what he'd been saying to the Russian all night long. "In the morning I'll go down the list and everyone you're the slightest bit nervous about I'll call. HIAS, Updegraff at Children's Services, whomever. It'll all be squared away. Even though none of it's really necessary."

"So don't call," Vitaly said without hope.

"Do you understand that there can't be an official record of an incident that hasn't officially been recorded? It's been forgotten about. Mrs. . . . Judge . . . look, it's been *settled*. Even if Gelman wants to make something of it, he won't be able to."

Vitaly raised his head. "The redhair steals from you, you knew this?"

"You overheard Bennett? I didn't think we were speaking that loudly."

"To my heart"—Vitaly raked fingers through his hair before sincerely touching one of his ribs—"you are only true friend for me. You won't like this—but you can be schmuck too. Everybody to take, the word? . . . *Meilah*."

"Merchandise? Advantage?"

"She comes to store at night, carries boxes away. First time, I try to stop her."

"What did she say?"

"Fucks me." Al began stuffing the pillow into the slip.

"You said it back to her I hope."

Vitaly shook his head in sadness. "Like my father." Sitting forward, peering into Shapes's eyes with the pride, even nearly the glamor of a person surprised by nothing, who's forced to deal with a universe of the helplessly naive: "She steals from you. But at least you fuck her, right?" When Shapes didn't answer, Vitaly keened sincerely, *"Don't* fuck her? Why not?"

Shapes turned his head to hear if the shower still ran, and thought it did. "I'm sure the one blanket will suffice. If you'll even need that." He stood and began backing from the room.

"Mad at me be, okay," said the Russian. "But I am like her—*bad. Do you fuck her?"*

"She's a friend of mine," Shapes whispered. *"And* of yours, as you saw tonight."

"No—the redhair! And Monte too!" His frustrated eyes raked past the walls, the Levelors. "Steals from *you!"*

"Bennett just informed me."

Vitaly slapped the pillow angrily. "So if she steals, you should fuck back! *Every-one* she does! *Me*," he jabbed at himself. "Fucks me! But takes from you *boxes* too!"

In the bathroom the shower spray was being turned off.

Shapes waited most of a week before going to see Iris at her house, in her exile. Earlier, on the phone, he'd said only that he was interested in discussing elementary sign-language lessons with her, nothing about the kids firing her. Yet her first words, as Shapes got out of the Volvo up by the house, were: "I knew you'd be here eventually, Charles, and it would all be straightened out." She clutched his hand with both of hers. "It was a misunderstanding and I'm holding no bad feelings toward either your daughter or toward Ben. Come."

"This is quite something," said Shapes. Right behind her, in step, marching directly into a nebula of gnats swirling like silent noise, he noticed that even the bottoms of her bare narrow feet were faintly tanned. The path she led him down was floored by bark chips and lined with low gray plantings; antique gaslight poles in different heights and styles, converted to use flame-shaped electric bulbs, stood here and there.

At the bottom of one branch of the path a pool of water evenly reflected a blisterish sky. A cuticle of sand served as a small beach, and it was here that Iris put herself down. But when Shapes lowered to the sand also, she quickly bumped away, putting six or so feet between them. (Sign-language lessons, Shapes remembered.) "Ben's *so* porous," she immediately started in again with, rising to a squat, hanging both wrists between her knees. "A lot of music people are. Even you a little—whatever you hear, you *listen* to. And you know what I think that's a symptom of."

The balls on this woman! Magnificent. "Bennett is claiming," Shapes began, "that a good deal of equipment, many hundreds or even thousands—"

"Oh, I wish he'd come out with you." She contemplated the middle of the pool with a visionary expression.

"He already was here."

"With Polk, I know. That must have been upsetting for him. Polk's down in Baltimore now for a while, by the way." She shook her head: "Possessions, possessions—even a spiritually free-ish person like you has a major hang-up about them."

"I like that: 'free-*ish*.'"

Iris leaned forward. "What is in your pockets now? Tell me exactly."

"Change," Shapes said, going along for now. "Loose bills. My new blood-pressure medication."

"*Both* pockets, right and left?"

"A set of keys."

"Could I have those?"

"Are we trading them for something?"

Iris got to her feet and walked around to the far end of the oval pool. "Throw them."

"They'll land in the water, Iris."

"Then throw them hard."

"What am I getting in return?"

"Oh, you'll get it. Maybe not as much as you've been thinking you'll get, but enough. Don't worry about that now—throw."

Shapes, still sitting, had to throw them underhand, which meant the arc of release was bad; landing a little beyond the exact center of the pool, the keys chucked up a water-divot. Iris took on an expression of concern—"The water's been muddy lately too"—and Shapes grinned, sure she was joking. But she went on: "We have a net up at the house, so don't worry. I'll find them sooner or later." The decorative pools were so obviously a few feet deep, lined with blue plastic. Shapes could even *see* the keys. Then realizing a few seconds later that this, in her desperation, might have been her plan—

to use his keys (without a set of her own anymore) to return everything she'd taken, maybe at night, after closing—Shapes suppressed his smile.

She was coming over now to take his hand, to pull him to his feet. As they walked up toward the house Iris said, "Basically, you know, I was whispering just now." Shapes mentioned the beneficial effects of his new dizziness medication, but she had no use for that: "Don't be so sure that the metal of your *keys*—electrical interference—hasn't played a big part in it also. We've got wires, sort of, in us, remember. We can get jammed too. Especially from keys. Possessiveness has a huge force field—it's a lime color on Kirlian auras. It *does*, Charles."

"Did I say something? I didn't say anything."

Inside the house she ushered Shapes to a high-legged canvas chair, watching as he surveyed the mostly bare main room. "Your granddaughters probably go to a modular school too, don't they? They must. We're so lucky here, in that respect—lots of empty, adjustable space. Over there"—she pointed—"will be for testing. And the area next to it for wishing."

"Won't that be very expensive? You'll have to put in a number of sinks."

"*Wishing*, Charles—not washing. Wish-intensification. Something I developed myself from studying the black churches, which I think will work great with sens-imp kids."

"Iris—"

"You want to try and get the child to ask for something *smaller* than what he really wants. Something he'd like but maybe *after* something else he'd like more. Then you try cutting it down—get him wishing for something below the level of anything he'd actually *request*."

"The story of my life," Shapes commented genially.

"And you're one of the few people who'd recognize it, too. Here, I'll explain it to you, how it works." Whenever she leaned forward somewhat, her fronts swung into plain sight as the sundress gaped. "Think—right now—of something you'd like but in these circumstances wouldn't ask for."

Shapes, after a moment's thought, said, "*Griben*."

Iris sat down in the other chair—"As if I can't already guess"—and hitched her décolletage.

"It's a dish."

"I'm flattered."

"Food, Jewish food."

"A dish so complex that you'd never ask someone to make it for you, right? Okay, but what if I *did* assemble it for you?"

"No, not especially complex," Shapes said. "And not assembled, strictly. If anything, you make it less. It's cracklings, chicken fat cracklings."

"Fat?"

"The unwiseness," Shapes smiled, "is half the flavor."

She stood on her tanned feet in order to pace. "I just can't see the healing properties in that." Going behind him, leaning over, she cupped Shapes's ears. "You're hearing better without those keys." Then she kissed the top of his head.

"Iris, really I have to talk to you." Yet something additional was doing behind his back: her hands had come away and in their place dual softnesses were pressing at his neck. The hands only returned to hold Shapes's head still, to not let him move it.

"Antimassacre or whatever, your hair's still greasy," she was saying. "And since I don't want to get soaked also . . ."

"Am I truly not expected to turn around?"

"They're just breasts, Charles—standard equipment on women." When Shapes did finally turn she was knotting the undone straps of her sundress at waist-level. "But look all you want, until the novelty wears off. All right? Now can we go into the kitchen and let me wash your hair?"

"Iris, cover up."

"I want you to see what I can do for you."

"Only if you do it dressed. And my hair doesn't need to be washed, it's clean."

"I'm washing it, Charles. And I'll need to take this chair with us."

If in the end he went with her into the kitchen; if he acquiesced, let her wash his hair, it was only because he could think of no other way he'd be allowed to close his eyes. And closed they needed to be—in case he in some way physically reacted.

Or didn't. He couldn't say which might distress him more. On the night of Vitaly's rescue, Leona was reclining on top of Shapes's bed when he finally got back from his talk with the Russian. Tied modestly around her was his bathrobe, but Shapes chose anyway to sit on one of the boudoir chairs some distance away, from where he chatted awhile. Then Leona had sat up and put her feet to the floor:

"Don't feel like it, Charles? I wasn't sure if this was a good time. Would a camera help? By all means go get one. You know this happens to *all* men sometimes. It's temporary." She lay back on the spread. "I'm in no rush. I don't have to be anywhere. My sweetikins is in Coral Gables for the month at his sister's . . . Is *that* it? Oh, I hope not. Let me explain this to you: My sweetie's been disabled for a *long* time and I've had to have a life. Or is it maybe our friend out there? If that's what's worrying you, I'm *very* quiet. If you want, too, we can just take pictures."

A waste to be mourned. A great shame—to cramp the style of a born giver. But though the next night too she was at his door—late, tiptoeing past sleeping Al—it was the same story, Leona in the end reduced to holding up the vial of Antivert as well as the one of blood-pressure pills on Shapes's night table: "*I'm* sure it's these."

Which was why if an erection came *now*—prodded by Iris's soft snouts collapsing against his cheek, pressing to the corners of his tightly closed eyes—Shapes would have felt doubly terrible. Something cold—presumably shampoo—was being drizzled onto his scalp from left to right. "Are you writing something on my head, Iris?"

"You tell me." One tit was moving against the center of his eyelid. "Whatever you think, that's probably what it is."

Shapes struggled upward to sit: "Hand me a towel. You're wrong, Iris—" but she pushed him back down and sprayed him, rinsed him, after which a towel pitched him into darkness.

He sat upright again. "*Secrets*—not music, are what clog. Isn't there an easier way than writing on my head to tell me what you want to tell me?" But when he grabbed the towel off of him, there was no resistance. Iris was gone from the kitchen.

Shapes called out, "You're obviously so frazzled you don't remember things you've known for the longest time. Haven't you even kidded me about my double set of keys? You forgot? The others are right here now too, in my back pocket. And haven't you yourself told me, when you described this house and the property, that the ponds are artificial, a foot deep and lined in plastic? We've *talked* about all this, Iris. I'll tell you, I'm becoming disenchanted with this whole notion of inner lives, deep secrets." His neck, damp, was chilling. "They *leak*. You forget who you told what to. When."

Iris's return was in the nude. Totally nude—thighs, hips, flaming bush in addition to the freckled breasts. In one hand she brandished a plastic comb, yellow against her white body.

"Your hearing's been at least ninety percent better since you've been here. All I ask is for you to let me finish you off."

Shapes jumped to his feet in alarm. Water trickled down the side of one cheek. "As of yesterday—when the papers were done officially—Bennett and Amy are your new bosses. Or ex-bosses—it'll ultimately be up to you and them," giving his head a quick rub, holding the same towel out to her, to cover herself with.

She didn't take it from him. "All that has nothing to do with *us*, Charles—but of course you're right: no secrets." Touching one of her own nipples: "I said we'd trade and we'll trade. That whole conversation we had about celibacy was asinine. You weren't telling me the truth and I wasn't telling it to you. The truth is that we both have needs. Right?"

Shapes draped the wet towel carefully against an arm of the chair. "I'm not even asking to know *why* you took these things. I am saying that bringing back at least something—as much as possible—will help. You don't need my keys for that, either: I'll be more than happy to meet you at the Barn tonight and tomorrow, do all the necessary schlepping." Iris was now stepping toward him. Shapes inched back, his legs hitting the seat edge of the canvas chair; if it came to that, he was prepared to snap the towel at her. "But much as I'd like to, I can't give a firm guarantee that even making partial restitution will absolutely matter. Vogelsang's past problems, the degree of your participation then and now . . ."

Splotch rose on Iris's speckled chest, a chevron of it, and for the first time now she attempted to cover herself with forearms and hands. Her expression had changed radically. "No!—that's Monte, that's separate!" She followed Shapes into the main room and made a grab for his arm, pressing the plastic comb tooth-side in against him. "I'm only involved with the school."

"But I'm sure someone official is going to be interested in why a 'school' or whatever, a 'church,' is warehousing stolen property"—something said in order to get her full attention, yet which Shapes knew to be merely an empty threat. As, probably, did Iris, for Monte was one of Judge Leona's cronies, and as Shapes now knew only too well, Leona's tune was what the local band played. He was uncomfortably in debt to her himself, last Friday's conclusion to the Vitaly incident proving that beyond any doubt. A clipping (it had been slipped under Shapes's door) from the Peekskill *Clarion*, a quarter page huddling uneasily next to an ad for Mimmo's Farm-Fresheteria, Bananas All This Week 49¢. Beth Emeth Temple of Peekskill had announced that, effective immediately, it was voiding its contract with Howard Gelman, who had served part-time as its rabbi for ten and a half months. Following a credentials inquiry by the State Corrections Department—for whom Gelman in addition served as adjunct prison chaplain and counselor for Jewish prisoners—discrepancies in the original personnel application had come to light. Gelman's highest-to-date certification had been found to be a master's degree in Social Work from Temple University in Philadelphia. No rabbinical ordination was confirmed. Charges had not yet been filed in the matter, but Gelman had been put on indefinite suspension by the State Corrections Department and also terminated from Beth Emeth, where no one was available to comment to the *Clarion* at press time. Reading this, Shapes experienced a feeling utterly new to him: of having been *brutally* helped.

"Bennett tells me, Iris, that you've been stealing me blind."

She gave herself a shuddery hug and gazed away distractedly. "Well, what the fuck do both of you know anyway."

"Get dressed," Shapes suggested, "and we'll start bringing things out. My wagon holds more than you'd think. I'll take as much as I can back." Yet, instead, Iris walked up the steep stairs at the side of the room, one hand shielding her breasts, the other her behind.

Shapes, once down at the end of the path, found his keys with no trouble, they were reachable from the shore, no need to remove shoes and socks or roll his cuffs. His newly washed hair frizzed angelically in the humid warm air. What for a moment he thought was the sound of a car engine starting up by the house turned out to be a rogue sizzle of the tinnitus playing in his ears. As he climbed back up the bark-chip path to the house he could see Iris nowhere.

But then she appeared—dressed, leaving an outbuilding, her arms filled with cartons, heading for Shapes's wagon.

SEPTEMBER

14

"Beethoven."

Shapes nudged down the volume knob. "Positively. *Les Adieux*—one of the ones the name-givers gave a name to."

"French?"

"I think it translates as *The Farewells*." Shapes was glad to see Vitaly let go of the glove compartment for a moment, something he'd been nervously snapping shut and open for most of the ride. On a Volvo, this kind of repair ran an easy hundred.

"Stupid to name a music French. Numbers, okay—to tell this from this—but a French name is stupid."

This had become strictly their style now—Shapes the father who never in his life had had a right opinion or idea, and Al the pouty son, grouchier even than Bennett at his worst (and under similar circumstances, since Shapes and the Russian now spent most of all day with the other, overseeing the newly opened, but practically self-managing, U-Store-It, the mini-warehouse Shapes had converted the D-Lux Motel into after buying out the Hings). With Bennett Shapes had learned to understand carping as a kind of immature stage of freedom, to be accepted, if not savored. Yet Al was often a trial, letting nothing pass, raspberries not only at what Shapes had to say but at everything suggested by the narrow bit of American life he saw wedging through the U-Store-It. People paying to stash junk in metal-clad cubicles whole families in the bigger Russian cities would die to live in, as he more or less put it once.

Shapes guessed aloud that the pianist they were listening to was Serkin.

"Too fast," Al judged.

"It's Serkin all right; I think I even have the record. And I think I disagree—I like the tempo."

Al's hand went back to the glove compartment door. "Stinks. Completely stinks."

"You mean it? He'll be crushed to hear you think that. Look, you can disagree with how he plays a particular piece, but—"

"Makes the music sound *crazy*," Al said with a disgusted face, leaning his temple against the rolled-up window on his side. The suit he was wearing, purchased at Caldor especially for today, was a Farah, of inexpensive stretch material but natty enough. He looked decent in it, not too slumped over. The tie originated in Shapes's closet, the shirt (though not a suit shirt really) was the same one Shapes and Sidney had brought as a token of goodwill to the halfway house. The only item of apparel Al had on of any personal history was his Russian shoes, the pair allowed out of Khabarovsk with him: bulbous-toed oxblood brogans, homely as sin. Yet appropriate somehow since little Nina, the daughter (not at all little anymore, Shapes had learned to his surprise; in fact a part-time assistant-manager-in-training at a Wendy's on Kings Highway in Brooklyn), promised to be formidable; and Al, in shoes like this, might stand half a chance of holding his own ground.

"Only right player is Gilels. Gilels is right, others they stink."

"Brendel *stinks*? Lupu stinks? Ashkenazy?"

"Stinks!"

"*Boychik*, Serkin does *not* stink."

Al straightened up. "The music is crazy? No, I mean this—it's crazy?"

"Well, I'll tell you: they say that around the time this was written, Beethoven walked the streets with a notebook in his hand, whistling to himself, humming off-key and laughing wildly to himself. The opinion in Vienna was, yes, *meshhuge*."

"*Who* says? Who's this who? Someone *told* you? And Vienna— shit on Vienna! we come to Vienna they rip us all off!" Al reached for the radio knob, sending the sonata into a decibel-zone high enough to worry Shapes. The Antivert, the hypertension pills, the salt-free diet, the biofeedback—so far they'd kept a grapple-hold on the tinnitus (though occasionally Shapes would be aware of a pale echo, a grapeskin surrounding sounds—and he'd be convinced the heavy-duty noise, the tormenting stuff, was doing nothing but lying low, in wait). His ears were clearer, and therefore he was protective of them, lowering the volume.

The Russian was hostile. "The music is the music. Gilels is for the *respect*. If your father is crazy, every time you see kids of him you say *Hello, nice to see you, children of the crazy father*? Of course not!"

As he was slowing the car for the toll plaza at the Triborough Bridge, Shapes acknowledged that this was an old argument: "Putting the interpretation in front of the material, or vice versa. But nothing in life's guaranteed; music has to take its chances like everything else. If someone playing this did—I'm not saying Serkin— but *did* think it's crazy—"

"No, not allowed!" Al cried heatedly. "Music is bigger than person!"

Shapes dropped exact change into the hopper. "You're wrong. People go to concerts to hear *persons*. Beethoven—please stop that, the door's going to snap off—Beethoven himself was a human being. Who happened to write—"

"Shit on what Beethoven writes!"

"Then I must not understand. What I thought you were saying is that what Beethoven wrote is the most important thing. Yes? No?"

With an opened hand and flexed stub fingers Al made a gesture of fumbling yearning. "What crazy Beethoven *tries* to make! But even for Beethoven is not always *it*, okay? Understand? What Charles-shappes or Roitmann does, whatever—also not necessarily *it*, you understand?" Jumpy in his seat, he was trying hard, but vainly, to be patient. "You do what you *want* to do—but you are only person. And person is shit. You want to do It, okay? But It . . . maybe it doesn't want to be do-ed."

"*Done*—but what is this mystical *it* of yours all of a sudden?"

"*It!*" Al cried self-evidently.

"As in God? The God kind of supreme It?"

The Russian slumped and looked down at the water, up at the barred windows of the hospital for incompetents. "Shit on God! You don't understand, so forget it."

Shapes originally agreed to go to biofeedback sessions in the city because about everything else Dr. Siegel suggested had helped. Why not this too? Yet to move the monitor's needle down to the green sector, brain waves grunting through wires attached to muscles and pulses, to forget all inner and outer noise, this feat took Shapes three and a half weeks, session after session of failing to budge the needle out of the red. How to empty your head of unnecessary kapok? When it occurred finally—a needle quivering in the green—elated tears had sprung to his eyes. After she unhooked him, he hugged the sweet young technician, Marybeth, and invited her out to lunch.

They ate pizza in a trattoria beetled by construction scaffolding for an office tower rising next door. Marybeth hailed from Alabama. She and her husband had been missionaries sent from their last station—in Africa, in Burundi—to work in a church-sponsored drug-rehabilitation center on the Grand Concourse in the Bronx. But six months into it the husband, Kirk, had vanished, to reemerge later in Kansas City, working in a Christian bookstore—in no emotional shape, the mission headquarters in Dallas reported to Marybeth, to resume the marriage just yet. They offered to bring her back to Texas or to Alabama, her choice, but months went by and no airline tickets ever arrived.

She had a circle of guardians on Fordham Road—a group of the cured addicts: Angel, Tio, John—who watched over her. And she'd secured a job in the city, as a secretary at McGraw-Hill. But finally she left the Bronx after an incident on the subway (which with an abashed look she said might have upset her more than it should have). She was on a downtown train, late to work in mid-morning, when a man in a heavy overcoat walked into the otherwise empty car and sat down opposite her. He began to fuss with the coat. Something with a small white head peeked out from one of the pockets—

Putting his hand over his mouth, and with the restaurant's paper placemat—a map of Italy—adhering to his elbow, Shapes had groaned: "Oh no."

—which turned out to be a mouse. Named Burt, the man said. His "co-worker" in the virology lab at Presbyterian Hospital. When the man said *Go!* the mouse started scampering from one pocket of the coat to the other, burrowing down, turning around inside the pocket and sticking its head out once more. Did Burt maybe want to be petted on the head by the nice lady?

After answering an ad in the newspaper for a roommate, she

moved from the Bronx to Elmhurst, in Queens. Emmy, the roommate, worked at the Biofeedback Center on Thirty-Third Street and she urged Marybeth to apply for technician's training. So here she was. And Shapes left the trattoria in love.

From the various social-service agencies involved with the case, Shapes had discovered that the daughter never actually believed the letters Al claimed Gelman urged him to write—the ones mailed to Gelman's acquaintances in different parts of the country, then to be forwarded on from there, attesting to Al's odyssey in search of radio-engineer work. He learned too that Nina the daughter wasn't necessarily unhappy with the status quo either: whenever a visit had been arranged in the past year, she'd called back the next day and pleaded stomach troubles. The social worker now assigned to the case, a Mr. Updegraff, saw it all as a stalemate and seemed to get tired the minute the subject came up.

"Don't look at *me*—I don't force the issue ever. I've had serious doubts from the start that this case is worth half the time I spend on it. We shouldn't even have an open file on it; they seem happy enough with how things are. This man of yours is a little strange and Nina's got quite a tongue."

"But you do understand," Shapes had said firmly. "Rosh Hashanah, after all."

"There was agreement from the girl and from Roitmann when I spoke to him. I repeated the date specifically a number of times, which you have to do with these two, the language and all. So they both had ample chance to reject it, to suggest something else. They said this one was fine. Now all of a sudden I'm the bad guy. They're calling from HIAS and now you." There was the sound of two sheets of paper being exchanged. "You maybe ought to take it up with the girl and the father, because I'll tell you something: I'm not letting this be *my* fault."

Surely there was some alternate date, Shapes said. But Updegraff in turn wanted to know whether there wasn't some alternate *driver*—no one else in the whole world who could drive Vitaly down to Brooklyn on the agreed-to day?

"Can I please speak to your superior."

"Everyone thinks he can squeeze out a little something better. Must we play games here, Mister, uh . . ."

"Shapes, *Rabbi* Shapes."

A pause. "Well, I wish you'd said. Don't go anyplace, you'll be speaking to a Ms. Occhiogrosso. In fact, give me your number in case we get cut off. That'll happen around here." A moment later: "This is Diane Occhiogrosso."

Shapes recalled once selling a spinet to an Occhiogrosso, a youngish couple. "And this is Rabbi Chaim Shapes from Goshen." The presumption left him feeling odd but definitely better—smoothed, unwrinkled.

She was very sorry, the supervisor said, that Rabbi Shapes had been caused such understandable distress. Was there a more acceptable date he had in mind?

"I hope not Yom Kippur!" Shapes barked kiddingly.

Poor nice Ms. Occhiogrosso had tottered down into herself as if draining. "We'll do our best to avoid that, Rabbi. I'm going to see what can be done and call you right back. Will you be at that number?"

"Sitting here right by the phone."

"And the names again are Roitmann? For both?"

"Nina. And Vitaly."

In Brooklyn, on a sidestreet, Vitaly cried: *"Ehteh!* There!"

Shapes hit the brakes near the corner. "Who? What? Nina?" All he saw in the vicinity was the back of a woman in a shiny purple quilted coat despite the continuing warm temperatures. "Do you want me to honk? Let her know we see her?" Shapes began to coast at a very low speed.

"Toorn!"

"I don't know what—" but Vitaly lunged and was wrenching the wheel, the Volvo's right front tire scraping against a section of curb, the car jouncing as Shapes struggled to captain it.

"Don't do that again!"

"Fuck you, Shapes! Stop car! I get out!"

Shapes steered back into the middle of the street, picking up a little more speed. Once he crossed the intersection, he roared down the next block and at the stop sign the car's squeal sent a knot of sparrows off a lawn, directly *up*, using no horizontal air. (Such a self-congratulatory big deal he had made about his peelings-back, Shapes thought, and here ordinary birds rise without fuss directly into the high. What good was inner spaciousness if it didn't buoy you, keep you aloft?) Shapes on the next street found a spot at the curb and pulled in.

Al, after his outburst, was now quiet. "I know this isn't easy," Shapes said as the Russian sat there unmoving. "Any daughter is a good deal to handle. But it's a first step." Vitaly began to push at the skin over his left jaw. "For as long as you want and need to be, you're my manager at the storage warehouse—so you have *stability* to offer her. For the first time in who knows how long. She'll appreciate that, you'll see. But whatever happens today, it's only a first step, remember. And we'll see it through together." Shapes started to pull away from the curb. "A tooth hurting?"

Inside the Wendy's on Kings Highway, Al stood uncomfortably studying the wall menu and poster-sized transparencies, trying not to meet a face, while Shapes asked the young girl taking orders at the register if he could speak to the assistant manager. When she called into the microphone, "Louis, come to the front, please," a short black man appeared.

"My error," Shapes told him. "I'm looking for Nina Roitmann."

Louis Gates (according to his gold managerial namepin) said, "So am I, my man." He nodded diagonally to the register girl to take care of the other customers, and she peered behind Shapes at Al: "Welcome to Wendy's—may I help you?" Flustered, the Russian might have been about to order had Shapes not pulled him clear. "No, we're together." To Louis Gates: "She's not here then, I take it?"

"She's swing—trainees always are. Today she comes on at one. Did you tell me who *you* are?"

Shapes drew Al forward. "This is her father. They had an appointment to meet here at two o'clock."

"You people been out all afternoon?" the manager said to Al. "No one answered when I called before."

Shapes interceded. "His English isn't so good. Tell me, is she usually on time?"

Back outside on the street, drowned-looking and worrying his jaw, Al bitched weakly: "See? Drag me?! See?"

"We're here already, let's give her a little more time." Shapes stole a peek at his watch. The kid was standing them up, no doubt about it. In the car, they drove around the block and parked near the end of a bus stop catty-corner to the Wendy's—to see if and when she arrived. In silence they sat, ten, fifteen, and twenty minutes, the Russian continuing to sand at his jaw, to rub too at his left breast on occasion. After a squad car came aside, the non-driving cop sending Shapes a quizzical, city-intimate look of *So?*, Vitaly gave a spasmodic fidget (with all the potential of an all-out *duck*) and Shapes then thought better of waiting there. He glided forward into traffic, the cop car right behind for a little while. "We'll have to circle."

It was too much for Al, the last straw. More whitely anxious than ever, palping his jaw fiercely, now he was massaging his shoulder too.

"You okay?" Shapes asked.

Grabbing at his chest, Vitaly complained of serious thirst.

Shapes drove a good deal faster. Al yelled, but Shapes said yet more urgently, "How's your stomach—any nausea?" A small private hospital was on Kings Highway, Shapes recalled, but would they have an emergency room? If they did, would it be adequate? Kings County maybe in that case. But that was far. Coney Island Hospital? Shapes, beginning to sweat, was feeling faint himself. "Al, do you want to get over to Coney Island Hospital and let someone look at you?"—recklessly making a left from the wrong lane to get on an eastbound street.

"Only need some water!" When the car stopped at the next stop sign, Al started to open the door handle. Shapes crushed the brake pedal and leaned over to keep the door closed: "No, not again! Close that door!"

"Give me drink!"

It was only then that Shapes saw where the car was. Realized what was only around the corner. And in that case, telephoning paramedics might be smarter than driving the streets himself. "I'm going to try to get you a drink, Al, but please sit tight another second or two. Where would you say the pain is? In your chest? Your jaw? Shoulder?" Moments later he had pulled halfway up the specific driveway. Vitaly looked at him. "Sit a minute," Shapes said, and got out.

Not wanting to see the block or anyone on it, Shapes fixed his eyes straight ahead at the storm door with its eagle crest, inherited from the previous owners when Shapes had first bought the house. Though now there was a different mailbox, replacing the one he'd shopped carefully for and finally found in a catalogue (he hoped it had been substituted for, not stolen).

No one was answering the bell or his knocks. It was very possible that someone entirely different lived here now, for Goolsby would have retired from his day job as a subway motorman and also probably from supering the apartment building across the street. Shapes had originally favored selling to the family for no more complicated a reason than as a way to help them up out of that wet, dark tomb of an apartment-building basement, its subterranean hive-apartment right off the puddled nook of washing machines and dryers and the banks of gray gas and electric meters, the skin-crawling kingdom of mice and pinky-sized waterbugs. Goolsby had knocked on Shapes's door the day the realtor's lawn sign went up—and was Shapes, Mr. Peeling-back, going to refuse a family poking out for light and air, for more space? Eventually he even offered a seller's mortgage, but Goolsby pridefully refused.

Shapes rang the bell a last long time and was about to turn away and come down the steps when the inside door pulled open and a shirtless black man wearing only a running-suit bottom peeked out.

"Yah? How you cahnt hit daht buzzer daht give a man some peace, huh. I know you?"

Shapes stared through the glass storm door at the man's hairdo, a bizarre, baked-looking mass of cigar curls. Then at the smile that slowly was trenching the sleepy face: "I do. I do!"

"*James?*"

"Mahn, you doan let me sleep!"

Shapes tamped air at pants-pocket level. "You were this big!"

"De way a tings," and an even toothier smile. "*You* used ta be *big-gah*."

"I've got a problem, James. Someone is sick. I'm afraid it's something heart. We were in the neighborhood, not far from here, and he's *begging* for water."

"Is what I gettin' him, den." James turned, showing the levees of a muscular back, but then froze. "Stupid, mahn, stupid—I and I play de arse. Bring him in here."

As pale, but now definitely curious, Al looked slightly better. Shapes opened the driver's-side door for introductions, but James came around to Al's side, opened the door, and without formalities grabbed hold of the Russian, drawing him from the Volvo in one torquing motion. Al in turn—in his best victimized manner—turned into a sack of unresisting bones, guided up the steps by James, who twice waved away Shapes's attempts to help.

The living room, where the Bechstein had once sat, had been repainted the color of a drink containing grenadine. Shapes thought it looked fine. The furniture was low and pillowy, the primary piece a sofa made up of long floor cushions without a bottom frame. Al was steered and deposited there while James went for a glass of water.

He sucked down much less of it than Shapes would have thought. "Your jaw," Shapes said, "do you have pain there still? Your shoulder?" Al awkwardly tried to cross and recross his legs on the cushions but said nothing. Then Shapes was being beckoned into the kitchen by James.

"It look so you panic 'bout he heart fah more den emergency. He instead seize up by some false fear, ya know?"

"Why are you talking this way, James? Can you tell me?" James's mother was the one with the most pronounced island accent in the family; his father had much less of one; and James himself—student-body vice-president of Midwood High—used to have none at all.

James conceded. "Tell me the problem," steering the subject back.

Shapes in a whisper provided a summary of the day's events. "So maybe he should be looked at nevertheless." Through the glass doors separating kitchen and dining room was visible an impressive array of electronic equipment, set up where Elise's oval dining table and walnut chairs had once been.

"I take he pulse when pullin' him out de car, mahn. Normal. Hyperventilation. Doesn't have other consistent indications of an infarct." Shapes again looked at him quizzically—and with equal confusion at the machinery in the dining room. James explained: "Where I work. Freelance biomedical. Decision trees. Wild stuff, mahn."

"You won the Westinghouse contest in high school, I remember. Decision whats did you say?"

"Honorable mention in the Westinghouse," James grinned. He

told Shapes that in his third year of med school at Columbia he'd realized clinical medicine wasn't for him, but that all this—pointing through the glass doors at the computers—was. "Artificial intelligence. Why I *know*, mahn, that your friend out there is having an anxiety attack only. His teeth are almost chattering."

"Medical school and you dropped *out*?"

Amiably indicating the keyboards, the monitors, the file cabinets, the stacks of folded paper, James said, "More creative. Also"—he fingered one of his hair-batons—"on account of my ways, more workable."

"I noticed. The accent, the *payess*."

"I make de nastiness bout *your* fait?"

"How are your parents, tell me."

"Me muddah taken where long time she want to go, mahn. My father didn't wait too long after to go back home: retired, took the Transit Authority pension, bought himself a house on the island."

"James, she *died*?" When the young man nodded—the identifiable Goolsby-family dignity: simple facts less than simply accepted—Shapes exclaimed, "I'm so sorry. A wonderful woman! All those years of doing a super's job during the day, fixing faucets. Everyone loved her. I was so fond of both your parents. I'm *very* sorry to be hearing this."

"The house," James changed the subject. "Looks different to you?"

"It looks *good* to me."

"Regrets?"

Shapes made his "Never" definitive: "Never *never* about this at all."

"You took heat, mahn."

"Better than giving it. But to get back to right now—what do you think we should do? Take him to an emergency room just to be on the safe side?"

"Your friend, you mean? That's up to you."

"I'm not the medical student. By the way, is this leave you took from Columbia temporary? You're not totally out, I hope."

"Maybe so, maybe not—my decision. Up in the air."

"Don't burn any bridges, James, please."

"I'll go take a second look at your friend now, Charles-mahn."

"While you do, I'd like to make a phone call."

"Your house," James smiled.

After dialing the number of the Biofeedback Center, Shapes looked around the kitchen. It was a tribute to his subscription to *Consumer Reports* (yet said something too about the Goolsbys, their thrift and care) that the appliances were the identical ones he'd left, although the refrigerator sported a color-splashed poster of a lion crest, an emperor's photo, and various hortatations in different flowing scripts about Babylon and powers, thrones, and dominations. Shapes couldn't resist: stretching the phone cord, he stepped over to crack the refrigerator door quietly. In the glare of the bulb, the shelves disclosed merely a squeeze jar of Hershey's chocolate syrup, a heel of cheese, and a few sealed Ziploc bags of chopped parsley. He shut the door.

For all that, though, it still was a perfectly bourgeois kitchen—not in any way part of the shambles, the hut, the nightmare of degeneration and squalor that he the selfish destroying lousy pigbastard *shonda* was accused of introducing to the block by Gloria Abron or the Starks or Milt Spicehandler: *What right do you have to give a whole neighborhood away? Who the hell do you think you are? The Social Experimenter?* Where were they now, those furious ex-neighbors, and when exactly had they fled? It was something Shapes didn't know how to ask James.

The receptionist at the Biofeedback Center told him Marybeth was with a patient right then. Shapes went ahead and cancelled his appointment, asking that Marybeth be told that he was all right, that he'd call back as soon as he could.

Vitaly, in the living room, looked like another person. Pallor gone, no grimacing, and the glass of water near him on the bare, white-painted floor remaining only a quarter drunk off. He was nodding gravely, but contentedly, to the exaggerated bumpiness of the music James had on.

Shapes lowered himself with difficulty down to one of the tuftings. "Not exactly *Les Adieux*"—a finger raised toward one of the four top-of-the-line speakers bracket-mounted near the ceiling—"but not the worst thing I've ever heard either."

James said, "It say de significances, Charles-mahn."

"I'm sure. But turn it down a smidge. Or else talk up a little. Al will vouch: My ears have had some problems lately. And that *accent* . . ."

"Whose?" James said impishly. "Al-mahn and I, we were talkin' about songs while you were on the phone. He appreciates the *beat*."

"Steady," Vitaly specified.

"It figures," Shapes nodded, explaining to James: "A conversation we were having about music in the car coming down here. Al doesn't care for surprises." (Which, now that Shapes thought of it, was something Iris had said during one of her anti-music diatribes on slow days at the Barn: that music has a way of making a surprise out of the least surprising thing there is: time. "As if you stuck a bomb into a length of pipe, Charles.") "We were listening to a Beethoven sonata and I liked it and he didn't. *Vigorously*. Al has a concept of the Ideal that's for me a little mystical."

James's eyes brightened at the word. "Too pure, those sonatas." Getting to his feet and lightly swaying, James sang along now to the record:

> *Hea! Mr. Music why don't you wanna play*
> *Don't you know today is a bright holiday*
> *Some people waiting for the message that you bring*
> *They listening to every word that you'll sing*

—while in the meantime Vitaly heeled-off his Russian clodhoppers. James sat down. "Music needs *words*, mahn. *They're* the ideal. Community, ya know? Everybody using the same jaw motions.

Watch singers lookin' at each other right in the eyes while they sing. No embarrassment. It can't be managed otherwise, neh?"

Shapes, who could smell Vitaly's socks, said, "That's fine when life's a chorus, James. But there are times of individual terror."

"Think so? *Nothing's* original, Charles-mahn."

"All right then, private."

James compromised: "Recapitulated."

Shadows were enlarging on the translucent paper shades covering the windows. Shapes's watch read 3:30. "Do you mind if I make another call?"

"Your house, as I say."

"Right," Shapes laughed, rising. "And since nothing's individual anyway . . ."

He spoke into the receiver more quietly this time, his eyes playing over the backyard outside: the last seasonal tomatoes drooping on stalks tied to poles with red yarn. A pristine white metal table centered two white wire chairs. The old peach tree still looked fit. Told the story by Shapes, Ms. Occhiogrosso at one point held the phone away from herself to call through the office underranks: "Anyone? A Mrs. Shtern phone in to cancel the Roitmann VWP this afternoon?" Then: "It's the first we're hearing of it, Rabbi. Is Mr. Roitmann handling it all right?"

"I'm an innocent I guess," Shapes said to her, "but it never occurred to me frankly that the guardian might *prevent* the meeting."

Ms. Occhiogrosso tskked. "Please don't come automatically to that conclusion—though I understand it. Rabbi, it would be *very* unusual. Everything in the files says that the Shterns are straightforward."

"So where was she then? The thing I'm worried about is that Nina could have come to some harm."

"I certainly understand. And share the concern. Our procedure is to bring the police in after a certain time has elapsed. Automatically, totally taken care of on this end. But I have to tell you—and it's very unfortunate—but a good sixty or seventy percent of the time, *espe-*

cially with cases involving adolescents, one or the other of the parties chickens out or never had any intention of going through with the meeting. You can understand what Nina's—Nina is it?—what her emotional dynamics might be under the circumstances. It's more common than we'd like, but that's the way it is."

Turning away from the backyard window, Shapes could see sockfooted Al being given a dining-room demonstration of James's computers: this and that button being pushed and vivid colors and circles and bars and lines springing up on the various screens (as all the while both Al and James unconsciously wagged hips to the seesawing beat of the music). "We were supposed to meet her at the restaurant she works at. But even the manager hadn't heard from her."

"We'll follow up, Rabbi, rest assured. I know this is upsetting. Are you calling from someplace public? Then we should probably try to wrap this up for the moment. Can I make a suggestion? Assuming there's nothing wrong, nothing fishy, let's get back in touch, say the beginning of next week, to try to re-set a date. In the meantime perhaps Mr. Roitmann might want to see one of the outreach psychologists. We can arrange that, they're available in these situations, with these sort of cases."

"I don't know . . ." Shapes hedged. Ms. Occhiogrosso admitted that "the other rabbi" wasn't too keen on the idea either. "But I wish you'd think about it overnight. They can be of real help."

"I'm sure, but Mr. Roitmann will need convincing."

"The language barrier and all," Ms. Occhiogrosso concurred. "Well, we'll see, and I'll let you go now."

Shapes joined the other two in the dining room. James was explaining his work, *decision trees*, which Shapes probably no more followed than did the Russian. At one point Shapes had to interrupt: "You'll excuse me, but as we say in Babylonian" (James frowned), *"from dus macht mir a leben?* You support yourself this way? You'll have expenses when you return to med school. This lets you put something away *and* feeds you?"

"Enough, mahn, for my needs."

"Cheese and chocolate milk?" And though Shapes knew he shouldn't, there was no way he could not: "My daughter and son-in-law have an electronics store upstate. It used to be my store—stereo equipment—but now it's Valley Computer and my daughter Amy—remember Amy? Well, she's all grown-up now, has children of her own—she's even gone back to school, to learn programming."

The plaits of James's hair (they resembled sections of hawser) shook when he laughed as Shapes went on with his proposition. But he wasn't yet saying no.

"And when you *do* decide to go back to medical school, you could still probably work there part-time. I realize it's a good-sized drive back and forth, but you have a car, don't you? A sturdy, *good* car?"

Here he had to check himself. No, no car. A car will ruin it. The generosities Amy particularly resented, Shapes always was relearning (as recently as when he had installed the Hings rent-free in one of the shopping plazas in Lauderdale Elise had left him as unconverted property-interest), were the ones that brought her no specific boon. A job for James at the store was one thing—and possibly even a very used car for basic transportation—but not a Volvo. *People who are too generous*, she once had accused, *are compensating for something else that's lacking*. About which she no doubt was right . . . though what that something else might be even Shapes's inner life—the peelings-back, the spirit-spaciousness—left him no clue.

Shapes said, "Done thinking about it? Yes or no?"

"You first speak to your children there, Charles-mahn. Then talk to me again."

"Well, I'm taking that then as a yes," said Shapes. "Maybe we should have a toast. Water, preferably"—recalling the bare icebox.

"Sometin' bettah I have." James left for the kitchen while Shapes and Al returned to the living room and the pillow-furniture. Shapes asked Al how he felt, who asked in return: "Your house this was? He was telling me."

"Eleven years, three and a half months. No more pain in the jaw or chest?"

James was back, holding a tube of paper the size of a breadstick, which he gave a skillful twist. Only when he pulled matches from the pocket of his jogging bottoms did Shapes piece together the whole picture. He hiked a brow. "Such a good idea, James?"

"The best."

"I'm not sure about that at all."

Vitaly came forward on pillows (and with him the high odor of his socks). "We smoke this at garage on Twelfth Avenue all the time. In Khabarovsk even."

"Today, though? Should you?"

James gave the cylinder one final tightening. "Ya friend Al and ya self, Charles-mahn, ya see in dis weed burnin' how God trew down Babylon. Doan fight it. Ack-cept. For de great day His wrath it has arrived."

"And one anxiety attack a day—of wrath or not—is enough. Really, James, do you feel that this is—"

Al, his shoulders plowing ahead, declared: "I want to turn on."

James was setting the thing on fire. "And you, Charles-mahn?"

"I vote for sitting and talking instead. Tell me for instance, James, what happened to you, how you got involved in all this . . . *this*."

But James only took a deep draw of the jumbo cigarette and then walked over and handed the thing to Al. Shapes cried out in protest, but James in strangled tones said, "His fear, it's done with; he had it already. And I can ask the question too: what happened to *you*, mahn?"

"Nothing and everything." Disconcerted, Shapes sat back. "As much as *can* happen—but I'm not the one in this room wearing *pay-ess*."

"And did you *mind* things happenin'?" James smiled clemently. "No, you didn't—because you're not the type who minds. I liked that about you always: that you knew it wasn't for the choosin', *your* choosin'. So why is this any different? This is supposed to happen too, see? Well then: say to me, *I want ta turn on*, as Al-mahn's heart do know. Say it. Goan."

"I'll leave all the saying to you two fellas."

"And everything else too, it looks like—come on, Charles-mahn, say it: *I want ta turn on*. Become one and right with your rhythms. Like Al's heart: open and shut, shut and open." James now took the thing back from Al. "Yet actually it goes 'lub-dub' all by itself—like Toots he have a song sayin'. By itself." Pointing at Al and himself: "I an I know dis."

Coughing—yet with unmistakable excitement beneath the spasm—to have been rescued from his life by his daughter's cruelty! to have lucked into this unaccounted-for release!—the Russian urged Shapes, "Go on, Charlie."

Being called *Charlie* touched Shapes. Never ever, though they were shoulder-to-shoulder much of the day at the U-Store-It, had Al called him Charlie before. And so, with an uncomfortable mumble—"I want to . . ."—he half obliged. James promptly leaned in his direction. Shapes simply waved it off and saw James stick the thing back into his own mouth again. "Okay," said Shapes. "I sort of said it. What did it prove?"

"The mahn wants proof!" James hooed smokily as Al (high already?) began chanting *I want to, I want to, I want to* along to the rhythms of the music. "The words *are* the proof. You need words, mahn. Can't just *hum*, gotta sing!"

James offered the cigarillo again and again Shapes declined: "Let's leave it at me being the designated singer."

"Do we hear you singin'?"

"You asked for it—"

On top of old Smokeeee—

—Shapes undergoing the sound of his own voice as something foolish yet cleansing, similar to his feelings about a session in the green of the biofeedback monitor. It occurred to him besides: If Iris desired to train her deaf children to ask for something just beneath wanting, how in the world could she run down music, itself a perfect example of just that? Which reminded him, too, that he ought to call Marybeth again.

—*All covered with . . .*

How special, anyway, could this "on" they wanted to turn be? No, what he really wanted was to *eat*. A deli, a diner, Chinese—but something. He was starved.

Design by David Bullen
Typeset in Mergenthaler Garamond #3
by Wilsted & Taylor
Printed by Maple-Vail
on acid-free paper